D1526991

a ~bookstrings~ novella

SPINES & LEAVES

CHAUTONA HAVIG

PUBLICATIONS

Fonts: Adorn Condensed, Albino Lovebird, Berton
Cover Illustration: Joshua Markey
Cover Design: Chautona Havig
Edited by: Haug Editing and TWE Editing

The events and people in this book, aside from any caveats that
may appear on the next page, are purely fictional, and any
resemblance to actual people is purely coincidental. I'd love to
meet them!

FICTION / CHRISTIAN / WOMENS FICTION /
ROMANCE

Welcome to The Mosaic Collection

We are sisters, a beautiful mosaic united by the love of God through the blood of Christ.

Each month The Mosaic Collection releases one faith-based novel or anthology exploring our theme, Family by His Design, and sharing stories that feature diverse, God-designed families. All are contemporary stories ranging from mystery and women's fiction to comedic and literary fiction. We hope you'll join our Mosaic family as we explore together what truly defines a family.

If you're like us, loneliness and suffering have touched your life in ways you never imagined; but Dear One, while you may feel alone in your suffering—whatever it is—you are never alone!

Subscribe to *Grace & Glory*, the official newsletter of The Mosaic Collection, to receive monthly encouragement from Mosaic authors, as well as timely updates about events, new releases, and giveaways.

Learn more about The Mosaic Collection at:

www.mosaiccollectionbooks.com
Join our Reader Community, too!
www.facebook.com/groups/TheMosaicCollection
If you'd like to find out about monthly launch team opportunities, sign up at
www.mosaiccollectionbooks.com/launch-team

Dedication

Dedicated to Francie Nolan, Anne Shirley, Jo March, and all the other fictional girls who understood me and my love of books when no one else did—and to the authors who made them come alive for me.

One

Like polka dots on the barren landscape, the overly optimistic creosotes were the only vegetation he could see for… miles! Milton's GPS instructed him to make a right turn onto Highway 177, but self-preservation resisted. He shot a look at his parrotlet seated on the over-the-seat perch. "It's like I'm Bugs and am taking a right turn at Albuquerque instead of a left." He frowned, parked on I-10 without another vehicle in sight to complain, and stared.

"The 10," as Southern Californians called the interstate, had to be a safe bet. Worst-case scenario, he'd ride along until he hit… what? Needles? Phoenix? This scrubby, two-lane road didn't offer much reassurance. Then again, wasn't he going the wrong way for those? "Need to revisit the Luddite idea, eh?"

A horn behind him nearly sent Milton through the roof of his Land Rover. He shot a look in his side mirror and saw a tourist bus bearing down on him. With a right-hand signal on.

Feeling like Robinson Crusoe or William

Robinson exploring a "desert island" rather than a deserted one, Milton snapped on his turn signal and eased onto 177. "All right, Atticus. That review better not be exaggerating. I feel like I'm about to meet Charles Manson's gang or something. Didn't that happen around here?"

Atticus chattered and preened in turn, always trusting that Milton wouldn't lead them into anything *too* unsettling. How they'd do this desert thing in late May was another story. If there wasn't a good campground to hook up his trailer, his exploration of Joshua Tree National Park might just end before it began. "Won't do that to you, buddy. If I can't find you a cool place while I'm exploring, we'll just try Colorado Springs again. That was nice."

A dot formed on the road ahead. It spread into a few more. They rose up from the ground as if mountains—squarish, block mountains with a few random trees here and there to soften edges. "Poor things. Those trees are doing time at hard labor out here."

The little town of Tamarisk, not far from the Tamarisk Lake Resort, but apparently unconnected with that place, boasted little. A tiny grocery store, what looked like an abandoned post office, and some kind of leftover combination five and dime-slash-hardware store greeted him as he rolled into town. Next up, an "art gallery" that looked like it hadn't been open in decades, a motel that probably shouldn't be, and a diner that had a line of melting customers waiting to get inside. Across the street... his heart did a skitter-thump and nearly caused him to slam on his brakes. There, clearly open and with folks going in and out... Spines & Leaves Bookstore.

"It's official, Atticus. We're staying the night. Even if I have to get a motel room for you to sleep in. Look at that..." He rolled by so slowly that the bus behind him honked again. "That's a good-sized store for a little place like this, but then..." A swarm of pedestrians forced him to come to a full stop. This time, the bus did not complain. "Apparently the tourists keep it alive."

A hand-painted sign with an arrow to the right read, "Parking—buses and vehicles." Milton went right. No Albuquerque for him. Behind the row of stores, a dirt lot, devoid of even one tiny creosote, served as the parking lot. Once he'd pulled in far enough, the bus rolled past him and into whatever spot the guy wanted.

But at the far end, much too far for tourists who would complain about the walk in the heat, a lone tree—cottonwood, probably—provided a bit of shade. Just enough to keep his Land Rover out of quadruple digits by the time he returned.

Once parked, he turned to his pal. "Okay, here's the deal. It's too hot for you to stay in the trailer—at least until I find a hook up, so into the doggie carrier you go. Sorry."

Atticus gave him *that look*—the one that said, "If you'd bought the leopard print one like I said, this wouldn't be an issue."

Milton had not and would not. Plain white for summer. Black for winter. He pulled up the carrier, and if birds could huff, Atticus did. He also hopped into the thing, knowing he'd get a bite of red bell pepper as a treat. Every time his little friend took that piece of vegetable-like fruit from his hands, Milton could almost hear the bird shouting, "Sucker!"

11

A stroll through town would have to wait—at over a hundred already, neither he nor Atticus could manage the heat. "Good thing we're not women, Att... I swear, we'd have new wrinkles already."

With the line now even longer at The Yucca Diner—an unfortunate name in his book—Milton went straight for the bookstore, as if anything could have kept him out. Peeling paint around the door and trim hinted that it had either been far too long since it had been spruced up, or the desert was even harder on buildings than he might have imagined if he'd ever thought to imagine it. Whitish stucco arches provided some shade from the direct sun and painted on them—the ubiquitous Joshua trees.

Milton stared. *Spikey leaves on those things. Spiny, like urchins. Spines & Leaves... clever without going overboard.* It boded well for what he'd find inside. Atticus scolded, as if reminding him that a white carrier didn't repel *all* the heat, so with that tingle of anticipation that always accompanied his entrance to a new bookstore, Milton twisted the knob and pushed open the door.

Bookstores and libraries—did anything ever smell better? Each one unique and yet familiar, too. Milton inhaled to catch the nuances of this particular store—much like a wine or coffee sommelier would. *Pulp paper, ink, dry dust... not even the slightest touch of mildew, but there are a few faint traces of cigarette smoke if I lean over just a bit...*

He pulled a book from the shelf to his right. An old Phyllis Whitney mystery. One whiff and he smiled. *The baking soda trick didn't quite work on this one...*

A voice called out to him. "Be right there!"

Youngish, female, breathy. Out of breath from working hard, or did she come by it naturally? He swept his gaze around the room. It had been packed with tall shelving units anchored to equally tall ceilings, and most of those shelves were stuffed to the gills with what looked like new releases and second and third-hand copies all mashed together. The window had shown a few new releases as well, but without anything on actual display, the entire room looked more like a library than a store.

"Well, Atticus… I wonder what gems we'll find for the little libraries across the country this time…"

At least the store was well organized. It might have every shelf so packed that he feared breaking a spine while pulling out a book, but the "classics" section was separated into more than just author names. Instead of Hawthorne being next to Hemingway, each had been shelved by quarter centuries and then alphabetically. He found *Travels with a Donkey in the Cévennes* by Robert Louis Stevenson. A closer look brought a frown.

"Hi!"

Milton jumped and nearly dropped the book.

"Sorry…"

Tall, curvy, wide smile, and a tiny cleft in her chin that looked rather out of place on such an angular face. Long, silky, dark hair—was it dyed? He wouldn't know. No roots showed, anyway. One eyebrow rose in a slight point compared to the smooth one next to it, which gave the woman the appearance of questioning him.

She peered into his "dog case" and started. "Oh! Bird!"

Milton held up the carrier. "Meet Atticus—not

Finch."

"I might be in love…" If the woman's gaze had not been riveted on Atticus, Milton might have bolted. A blush formed and she sputtered, "With the bird. Is it a budgie?"

"Parrotlet."

"Miniature parrot?"

Something about that "miniature" always felt like "imitation" to him, but Milton just nodded. "They're the smallest member of the parrot family. Some call them 'pocket parrots.'" Okay, now he was just babbling. But the woman kept asking questions. As they talked, Atticus strutted, chattered, and preened. "He's a bit of a showoff."

"Oh, he's…" She winced at Milton before adding, "Sorry, but I have to say it. He's darling."

"I'd take umbrage. *He* will grant you permission to recognize his perfection." Milton held up the book he'd found. "Are these stock numbers or the price?"

"Price." She beamed and thrust out a hand before realizing his were both full and jerking it back again. "I'm Ced. Current manager of this tomb of trees."

The way she said her name made it difficult to know if it was "Sayd" or "Sayed." She didn't look Indian, and besides, wasn't Sayed reserved for Indian *males*? "Unusual name." That was usually safe.

"It's short—for Mercedes. My dad's a big Dumas fan."

"'Mercedes might have been a queen…'"

The woman's dark eyes widened. "You know Dumas."

Milton nodded. "I know books." He passed over the Stevenson book. "Will you hold onto that

14

for me? I have more excavating to do."

"Excavating!" Rich laughter with only a hint of breathiness filled the room. "That's brilliant. I'll have to tell Dad."

In that one short sentence, Milton discovered just what the young woman was doing running a bookshop in a semi-ghost town like Tamarisk. *Dad.*

"May I take Atticus to the counter and talk to him?"

After handing her the carrier, Milton pulled a small baggie of sunflower seeds from his pocket and passed it over. "He can have a couple of these if you want to offer him a treat."

Making kissing noises, "Ced" and Atticus disappeared behind the bookshelf and out of sight. Several shelves over, he found a copy of *The Girl of the Limberlost,* and at the price inside, held onto it. Claude McKay's *Home to Harlem* came next, followed by Smith's, *I Capture the Castle.*

Only when his stomach rumbled for the third time did he realize how much time had passed. The bell jingled. A masculine, if not deep, voice greeted Ced.

"Hey, Ceddie. Wha—whatcha got there?"

"A customer's... parrotette?"

Parro♪et. Milton didn't allow himself to correct her.

"Cute little thing. What's her name?"

"His—Atticus."

"Awfully pretty for a boy."

If he'd been nearer, he'd have explained about birds—how often the males had brighter, bolder plumage. Ced did it for him. "Ever see a pea hen?"

"A pea what?"

15

He inched his way closer to the front, listening as the well-educated Ced explained about the birds. "They're kind of grayish brown—except for a colorful neck. The boys, the pea*cocks,* are the pretty birds—vain and egotistical like most guys…"

Stepping around one more corner, Milton could see her talking with a guy… deputy or park ranger? He couldn't be sure. When Ced saw him approaching, she grinned. "It's…" she frowned. "I didn't get your name. Sorry. We got off on books and…"

Shifting the books under one arm, he thrust out his right hand. "Milton Coleridge."

Hand frozen just a couple of inches from her body, Ced blinked. "Are you serious?"

"'Water, water, everywhere…'" He shook his head. "Um… not quite apropos for here. How about, 'That willing suspension of disbelief for the moment, which constitutes poetic faith.'"

"I missed something." The man, on the short side, though definitely taller than Milton, and also what older, better-written books would have called wiry, shot out his own hand. "Marcus Mendez."

"Nice to meet you… deputy? Mendez?"

A nod preceded a grin that rivaled Ced's. "Good to meet you. What brings you to the S & L?"

So much for me thinking I liked you. Milton gave the man a smile that probably looked as tight and forced as it was. "We're driving through on the way to the park. GPS recommended that Yucca Diner— unfortunate name."

"Isn't it!" Ced laughed. "Marcus and Dad don't see why, but it's terrible!"

"It's a native plant. We're not *that* far from

16

Yucca Valley. Why shouldn't it be?"

Milton gave all attention to Marcus even as he passed over the stack of books he'd collected. "I'm in business. I know marketing. And generally speaking, you avoid words that have negative connotations. Yucca might be a delicious plant, but the first thing you hear is 'Yuck.'"

The man started to argue, but Ced wasn't having any of it. "If you'd first come to town and had a choice between an equally busy Yucca Diner and a Denny's, tell me you'd have gone for Yucca. I dare you."

That's all it took for the guy to surrender. "Okay, okay." Hands in the air, he winked at Ced, and anyone not standing a bit to the side wouldn't have noticed the tinge of pink behind her ears. Milton noticed.

"I'm heading over to our yucky diner. I promised to drop dinner off for Gordon. Want anything while I'm in there?"

A few people came in and began wandering around the room as Marcus spoke. Ced greeted them and turned back to him. "What are you getting Dad?"

"Burger, fries—"

Ced glared.

"Um… Salmon and rice? Broccoli?"

That glare turned into a smile. "And get him some ice cream." She turned to Milton. "They make the *best* ice cream. There are two full-time employees whose sole job it is to keep the freezers going."

"I'll have to try it. I'm supposed to be over there, but I couldn't stand out in that line with Atticus. He'd get heatstroke or something."

At that point, Ced shot Marcus a pointed look.

He glared back. The look sprouted multiple daggers. He sighed and said, "Hey, Milt. Know what you want? I'm bringing back an order for Ced anyway. Can't let a little guy like this get overheated…" He poked his finger at the mesh wall. Atticus nibbled at it, and instead of being annoyed, Marcus beamed. "Hey, he likes me."

After a few suggestions, and several arguments between Ced, Marcus, and a few of the customers as to what would be his best first meal from the Yucca, Marcus took off with their orders, and Ced rang up a couple of book sales. Less than thirty bucks later, the store had emptied again. Her sigh told him it wasn't enough.

His original idea shifted. After another glance around the shop, Milton made his move. "Can you add up the total on those books? Don't ring them up… just give me a rough estimate."

"You're looking at…" She set down the last two. "Around fifty dollars."

He pulled out a hundred-dollar bill and laid it on the counter, covering it before she could take it. "I wonder if you'd consider a bet-slash-proposition?"

"What kind?"

Milton slid the Stevenson book from the pile and pulled out his phone. "If this book has *sold* for less than seventy-five dollars on eBay in the last six months, I'll give you a hundred for the whole stack—that's double your estimate."

"And if it sold for more?"

"You'll take this stack and do some research on them while I pull a hundred books off your shelves—books that I guarantee you will never sell. I buy them for a hundred dollars, you get space…" He hesitated as she took in his words. Should he do it? A spark in her eye caught his interest. Hope.

Milton turned another page in the book of his life. "…and let me see what I can do with the extra space."

Two

When she'd walked out to find her newest customer standing there holding a dog carrier, Ced had instantly labeled him as weird. In her experience, the only people who carried those things were over-processed women trying to look and act like they *thought* celebrities did. Those women would totter into the shop in their stiletto heels, with their pampered pooches in designer carry bags, realize there were no couches or lattes, and strut right back out into the heat. Seconds later, another luxury vehicle would roar down the road, back to the 10 and civilization.

It was exactly why Ced would never serve coffee in the shop.

"You know... a hundred books don't take up nearly as much space as you'd think..."

A woman carried a book of nursery rhymes to the counter, cooed at Atticus, and made a comment about how few books there were for children. Ced apologized as she pulled the book closer to ring it up. "Sorry... we don't get many children in here. I do think there are a few picture books that just came in.

Would you like me to get the box?"

It was a waste of time, of course. Curating a good collection of children's literature and picture books when you know nothing about them is harder than any other genre. The woman would ask—

"Oh, that would be lovely…"

Yep. There she goes. She'd pull out the box, and a moment later, the bell would jangle as the woman left with only the book of nursery rhymes.

Except it didn't happen that way. The woman pulled out two picture books and a children's novel—some middle-grade fantasy adventure she hadn't remembered ordering. "I'd like these. They'll be perfect."

Not until the doorbell finally did jingle did Ced realize that the man, Milton, had faded into the background. She wandered around the store and found a few odd stacks of books in every row. Though most could be found on supermarket bookracks, she did see a couple of poetry books, a few Dover classics, and that historical romance they'd just made into a BBC series.

"Mercedes?"

"Yeah?" she called back as she hurried his way.

"Would you have any boxes? It would be easier if I had boxes."

She did a circuit back to the "box room," and arrived with three in hand. "I'll go drop the other two near some of the other stacks." But she didn't. Ced watched as he stacked *Dracula*, Anne Rice, and *Twilight* all in one box. Added to that were a few erotica titles her father hadn't meant to buy. He'd rejected the pile of Christian fiction meaning to take those and refuse the "torso books." Never able to

22

toss a book no matter how much he despised it, he'd shoved them to the top and back of the bookshelves.

"Secret penchant for steamy books?"

Milton gave her a look but said nothing.

He had a point. Anyone who could actually quote Coleridge probably wasn't into books describing steel abs and other impossible physiques. "So… what will you do with all this? I'm not picturing you the…" Ced picked up the top book from the smut pile. "Um… *Hot Summer Knights* type."

"Most, I'll leave in little library boxes along the route from here to my next stop. Those…" He nodded at Mr. Chiseled Abs, "will line Atticus' cage."

Ced clapped a hand over her mouth, but not before a giggle escaped. "Oh… oh, my."

He rearranged as he went, moving one row up, another row over, and so forth. At times like these, all Ced could think of were the words of Solomon. "I wonder if Solomon had any clue how true his words were." Yes, it was a test, but it was also true. She'd often wondered, and watching him move book after book… after book… after row…

"'The writing of many books is endless'?"

"Yes."

He turned and looked up at her from his position hunkered on the ground, hands and arms full of books. "'I guess there are never enough books.'"

"You and my father both!"

"And Steinbeck." Milton rose, three copies of *The Hobbit* in hand. "Mind if I take these three? There are six of this exact edition left…"

"Take three more on the house."

The guy did it. She blinked for a moment and

asked, "What about Steinbeck?"

"He's the one who said there are never enough."

Curious. As much as Ced loved to read, having worked in the store most of her life, she didn't think she agreed. "And your opinion?"

"I lean toward Browning. '"No man can be called friendless who has God and the companionship of good books."'

A Christian. Interesting.

Just about then, Ced realized what Milton was doing. Nearly an entire shelf had been cleared off with the constant shuffle and reshuffle of different editions and a few double-stacked rows of old Mickey Spillane detective novels. "What'll you put on that shelf?"

"The contents of the one just inside the door. We'll need to do some more rearranging, but…"

Something in his words snapped something in her. "Um, I agreed to sell you the books."

"And to let me see what I could do with the extra space."

"Why should I? What do you know about selling books?"

He shrugged but moved toward the front of the store. However, instead of going straight for the books, he went to the carrier. With a quick zip and a finger stuck inside, he pulled out Atticus before heading to the door. A quick look up and down the street prompted him to lock it and flip the *"Taking a smokeless break—don't want to ban or burn books around here."* sign.

Atticus marched up and down his finger until Milton lifted his hand a bit, and then the bird flew around the room in a circle before landing on a shelf near the ceiling. He swooped down just a moment later and circled another time. Mesmerized by the bird's grace and the sheer novelty of a bird in her shop, Ced forgot to be irritated that he'd just locked her door without even asking. Then it clicked.

However, before she could complain, Milton's entire body language shifted. He tapped his finger and said, "Come, Atticus." The bird flew once more, but at a second tap and call, flew right to Milton.

"Good boy... I think I have a pepper here..." He pulled out a little baggie with small bits of bell pepper and popped a piece into the carrier. "In you go." A second later, he unlocked the door.

One moment, that bird had circled her shop a few times, and the next, another customer walked in and missed the entire show. Less than a minute later, the customer left—as most did. Every year, fewer and fewer people stayed to peruse the shelves as they once had.

"I know nothing about selling books," Milton said once the door's bell quit ringing. "But I do know what makes a business successful or not. And I think with a few changes, that you agreed to, remember, we could convince people to linger longer. And the longer they linger..."

"Am I the only one who hears Dr. Seuss in that sentence?"

As Milton zipped up the carrier, he said, "Are you going to help me help you or not?"

Bossy... But for reasons she couldn't understand, Ced removed an armload of books from the shelf and took off for the empty one near the back.

When Marcus finally made it inside the Yucca Diner, Lupe caught sight of him and passed her order pad on her way to the food window. "Write it down."

A guy who looked like he'd just stepped off one of the PGA West courses began an under-the-breath tirade that even Ceddie could probably hear. "Why don't you just come in like that and push ahead of people who've been waiting out in the heat."

His wife elbowed him. Marcus wrote the ticket anyway. He knew better than to argue with Lupe and Brent. They'd give him all the wrong stuff just to make a point. Besides, inside fifteen seconds, the guy would be ordered to stuff it or leave.

The first scowl came in conjunction with that thought. Lupe straightened her back five seconds later. Turned at ten. Marcus frowned and scribbled faster. *Here we go…*

All five-foot nothing of Lupe appeared at the guy's elbow—or so it seemed. "If you don't like how we honor our LEOs, you can go buy a can of weenies at the general store. They might even have a cold can of something left. Otherwise, be quiet or leave."

"Hey!" The man blinked. "What's a LEO?"

Though he rarely got involved, this time, with so many people crowding in and out, Marcus decided he needed to say something before it escalated. In a calm, almost lazy move, he turned to the man. His tone, however, he kept as firm and commanding as possible without drawing more attention to them. "Law enforcement officer, and if you disturb the peace here, sir, I will arrest you. It's that simple. Don't

26

do that to the restaurant or your wife. Have some class." He shot a smile at the man's wife and went back to the ticket.

If a complaint came in, he'd be in trouble with his boss for starting off confrontationally, but Marcus knew guys like this. If you stood firm, and if you made self-important people doubt how people would perceive them, you had a chance. *Bluster or machismo?*

"Let's get out of here."

Your loss, buddy.

But the wife laughed. "Go right ahead. I did not risk heat stroke only to walk out because you can't show a little respect and appreciation for a man doing a thankless job."

Go, Myrtle! Her name was probably something like Stella, but he always thought of the feisty ones as Myrtle—unless they were under forty.

"Connie…"

Or Connie. Connie works.

"Done with that?" Lupe held out her hand. "Brent's got a perfect spot to slide it in. Give it over."

"If you add three half pints of ice cream—your pick—it is."

She shot him a grin. "How'd you know it was dulce de leche day? You *always* know."

Yeah! Though he shot her a grin, Marcus said nothing and backed out of the way.

A party of eight left, and a busboy raced to clear the table in a jangle of crockery and tableware. The clunk-clink of plastic diner glasses against the plates added a touch of percussion to the cacophony. In seconds, the tables had been pushed apart, and another busboy had them wiped down and ready. Two more parties got seats.

"We have room at the counter for three," Lupe called out as she passed with a tray. "Room at the counter for three, first in line first, please…"

Two bus drivers pushed past him, nodding as they passed. "Connie" and her husband were next up. Booth for two near the window. Perfect. Nice and far away from him. *Just wait'll you taste…whatever you order. I'm gonna bet the steak melt. Ask for your fries extra crispy, and you'll forget you had a wait.*

By the time Jordan, the busboy, brought out five bags, a third of the restaurant had already turned over. And the line hadn't shrunk at all. "Wish they'd buy those buzzers," the kid muttered. "Then people could wander around away from the doors while waiting. Sit in their cars or something."

He'd wished the same for years. Best he could do was call for a pick-up order, but then he couldn't always talk Ceddie into eating. When he managed that, Gordon was happy, which made them all happy in their own ways. *Your matchmaking isn't going to work. She's outta here the minute she can go, and I'm not investing myself in someone who'd want me to leave.*

Had she been staying, he'd have asked her out the day she arrived, but the only thing worse than falling for a woman you can't be with is letting her know you did. So, Marcus pretended to be put out whenever he *had* to include her in meal runs or poker nights. He pretended he didn't love every minute of it. He pretended his heart wouldn't ache when Gordon could take over the store again, and she could go back to San Diego.

The oven-like heat nearly suffocated him the moment he stepped into the street. Cars and trucks braked as he made his way across to the Spines &

Leaves. Most waved. People could say what they liked about Californians, but folks were pretty much the same everywhere. California had just been defined by Los Angeles and the Bay Area instead of by the real folks who lived in the other ninety percent of the state. *It's like saying all of Illinois is just like inner-city Chicago, or all of New York State is like Manhattan or something.*

Pushing open the door of Spines & Leaves, Marcus called out, "Get it while it's hot." He dug through the ice cream bag, pulled out two containers, and began peering into the other bags to find Milt's and Ceddie's orders. The bird chattered at him as if demanding a bite.

"Ceddie?"

"Back here. Hang on. I'm holding books for Milton."

Holding books for Milton? *Shouldn't that be the other way around?* He turned from the counter and froze. Something had changed. It took a moment, but then he saw it. The bookshelf to the right of the door as you entered. Gone.

"Did someone steal a bookshelf?" Dumb question. "Or did Milt just break it?"

A thud answered him—a thud, a chuckle, and a giggle. Marcus had the crazy impulse to add, *"...walked into a bookstore..."*

Ceddie appeared first, with a slightly shorter Milton right behind. He hadn't noticed how short the man really was. Then again, Ceddie was kind of tall for a woman—five-nine, wasn't she? The appraising look he gave her confirmed his suspicion, prompted a raised eyebrow from her, and reddened his ears.

I might officially hate him for no logical reason at all.

"See how much bigger it looks in here!"

Milton pulled out his wallet and passed over a twenty. "Does this cover it?"

Ignoring him, Marcus asked Ced, "Can you break a twe—?"

The man threw up a hand as if a beat cop or something. "You went to get it. Keep any change, what little there probably is."

"Not allowed, but—"

Again, Milton interrupted him. "Donate the change, then. There has to be some local charity or county organization you can contribute to. Just don't let your food get cold."

"Feed me." The antithesis of the deep-voiced, creepy plant in that stupid musical, the bird's high-pitched voice still had an unsettling quality as it squeaked out, "Feed me!"

Three

Tammy's Tumblin' Trailers looked every bit as sketchy as its name. When Milton discovered that Tammy wasn't a person but rather a nod to the town's name, he'd almost opted for the equally sketchy motel. Still, there was something to be said for being murdered in your own bed instead of a stranger's.

He spent Sunday hiking around what parts of the park that were open. Who knew the "raptors" were nesting and that limited your options? Still, if his tax dollars were going to go to parks, he wanted the creatures to have a home. Especially birds.

Atticus had agreed. However, Milton suspected that was more due to the fact that he'd given the bird part of his mango. His plan for Monday had included another trek out into the desert—this time with twice the water and sunscreen. However, something drew him back into town, Atticus in tow. "Looks dead today, doesn't it? Hot, too. Already over a hundred." Heat radiated off the road. "Kind of reminds me of what Anne Lamott said. 'If you don't die of thirst, there are blessings in the desert.' So, we'll have to figure out what those blessings are, eh?"

He'd planned on the diner, but since there wasn't a line, he parked and strolled over to the bookstore first. Maybe Mercedes would like a shake or something. Wouldn't hurt to ask.

Mercedes. If he could stay longer, getting to know her would be interesting. There was something about that woman... Then again, she was a good two inches taller than him—curvy, too. He'd never cared one way or another, but despite the accusations women had thrown at him about how men always wanted to dwarf their women, in his experience, it was the other way around. Taller women hadn't been interested in shorter men. *Or maybe they just aren't interested in* me. *Probably that.*

The door jingled as he opened it, and Mercedes called from the back. "Be right with you!"

"No rush. Atticus and I just thought we'd wander around again—out of the heat."

A head popped out of a door at the back of the building. A grin. "Milton? You're back!"

It was the first time in the history of "be right with yous" that the person had actually appeared right away. She practically ran through the store. "Tell me what I did right and wrong. Seriously, I know something isn't right, but I'm selling more books, so I did *something*."

That's when he saw it. More space on shelves. Books turned face out in front of the ones behind them—just here and there, but the effect was already much more pleasing. "Whoa... I missed this." He reached for a Kafka and opened to the publication date. First edition. "This might be worth something. Better check it."

Mercedes blinked at him. "You're serious. I picked that because I thought the cover was bold—that red at the top."

Milton felt her eyes on him as he scanned the small but much more open area at the front of the shop. "You have a good start here."

"How do you know that? How do you know any of this?"

He stared at her, an idea growing before a decision made itself for him. Milton extracted his phone from his pocket and pulled up his website. The "about me" page. Passing it over, he said, "This is what I do. I save companies from being taken over or from bankruptcy. If you're worried, I can provide two dozen testimonials—printed and signed. Or, if you trust me, you can read half of them on the testimonials page."

The air grew eerie, with only the rattle and hum of a swamp cooler doing its best to keep the store at bearable temperatures to break up the silence. Milton expected a lone tumbleweed to roll down the main aisle in the store—maybe accompanied by the opening notes of the theme to *The Good, the Bad, and the Ugly*. Mercedes swiped, tapped, and as she did, she began to nod.

"Okay…" She passed over his phone and pulled out her own. After a couple more minutes of searching—his name, presumably—she squared her shoulders and asked, "Okay. Let's say I trust you. What else?"

"You need somewhere for people to sit. And that patio out there—with misters and a canopy? People could sit there and wait for a table at the diner."

"Oh… I hadn't thought of that."

"You could put a vending machine out there and make more per day in sodas than you've been making in books, I bet."

He'd tried to hide what he really thought, but she must have caught on. "What? What else? I see it."

What the store needed was a complete overhaul—both in arrangement, decor, and emphasis. It would take him a week to figure out the nuances, and both of them a full week to make it happen, and that was if she had the money to buy the few things they'd need. That canopy—not an option. A must. Tables—cheap from Walmart would work in a pinch. Even picnic tables would suffice. But the sofas… those would be expensive. And they needed that seating. Badly.

"How determined are you to turn this place around?"

Something shifted in her—demeanor, body language, everything. "I have a chance to stay. My boss…" She looked around her as if someone could overhear them. "He says I'm doing great remote work. That means I'd only have to be there for important meetings. If I stay…"

That made no sense. Stay? "You don't live here?"

Her silky hair swished around her shoulders as she gave a jerky shake of the head. "San Diego. I'm an accountant with a good firm. They don't need me there, and actually, my boss is thinking if I can figure out a flow, he could move us into a smaller building—everyone work from home. That way he could save money and increase salaries at the same time."

Two or three weeks. It could mean a straight drive from there to Delaware, no meandering, but to know he'd revitalized a *bookstore*. What could be more glorious?

Setting Atticus on the counter, he asked for a pen and a few sheets of paper. Mercedes gave him an odd look before snatching several sheets from a printer tray and pulling a handful of various pens from a jar under the counter. "Okay, now what?"

"How serious are you?"

"About saving Spines & Leaves?" She couldn't meet his gaze, but this time a suspicious sheen over her eyes hinted at why. "I grew up in this store. I fell in love with Ramona, Nancy Drew, The Outsiders, and V.C. Andrews in this store—don't judge," she hastened to add. "I was an angsty teen like most. I've improved my reading tastes over the years."

Milton shrugged. "One appreciates a fine steak much more after having had a dried-out, tasteless, fast-food burger."

"Yes! Thank you! My dad…" She sighed. "Dad had a stroke. This store…" Mercedes ran her fingers along the spines of books that stood behind the counter. "It's his life. And he's getting better, but if it doesn't make more money, he'll have to close it and move somewhere so he can earn minimum wage. Right now…" She tapped her temple as if it made sense. "I know numbers. Minimum wage and no expenses would save him financially and kill him in every other sense."

"What's my budget?"

"As little as possible." She winced as she said it. "I'll be taking from my savings, so I have to be careful."

In five minutes, four of which he spent calculating table space, Milton had produced a Walmart list. "We need this. Now. Like, *today*."

As she scanned it, Mercedes nodded, winced, and nodded again. "Why the standing ice chest?"

"We'll put it behind the counter for right now. People can buy ice-cold cans from you until we can get a vending machine out here. Put all funds from that toward the machine. Dollar a can. Period. And stock up if there's a sale that gets you soda for a quarter or less a can."

"Of course."

"I'm talking twenty or thirty cases of each flavor. Oh, and don't be brand loyal. If Coke is cheaper, you get Coke products. If Pepsi is cheaper, get that."

She grabbed her keys, and a Toyota logo caught his eye. "Tell me you have a Tundra or something."

"Prius." She laughed at the wince he knew he hadn't hidden. "No worries. I'm going to go get my dad's truck—old but runs great and can haul more than an old Ambassador car in Mumbai."

"I have the okay to start moving stuff?"

She hesitated… indecision graffitied itself on her features. Resolution washed it clean. "Definitely. Whatever you say."

"Got a source for couches?"

Another wince. "I'll steal Dad's until we can afford the time and money to go to Ikea."

"Great idea." He hesitated before adding, "Where's a key? I'm going to go get Atticus' cage. It's more comfortable for him than the carrier."

Wresting one from a ring with enough keys to open a chain of bookstores, Mercedes hesitated

36

again. "I *can* trust you, right?"

"I'm giving you what others pay tens of thousands of dollars for me to do. I don't need to steal your hundred-dollar till."

That wince would produce lines if she didn't stop it. She pressed the key in his hand, whispered thanks and an apology, and raced out the door. Milton picked up Atticus' carrier, checked to see the back door was locked, and let himself out. "Looks like we've just gotten our first pro bono assignment."

People were lined up outside the Yucca by the time Ced returned with a truck full of picnic tables, soda, and every banker box Indio had left. What he planned to do with those, she had no idea. Fifty had better be enough, though. At least the more expensive ones from Staples had been on sale. It brought them to almost the usual price at Walmart.

Three senior ladies, all sporting T-shirts that read, "I SEE NO REASON TO ACT MY AGE" in a scripty font, exited, laughing and talking as they strolled across the street. They all carried SPINES & LEAVES BAGS. What had he convinced them to purchase?

She pushed open the door, prepared for chaos, and instead, found two more women and a man waiting for Milton to ring up their purchases. One woman had a stack of quilt-themed mysteries by Earlene Fowler. Ced had peeked into one of those as a teen. It hadn't been bad. *Bet I'd like it now.*

The woman had a stack of assorted Georgette Heyer books, and the man had about every book on the Mojave Desert that they had in stock—no small feat. Not only that, another shelf had disappeared. Impressive.

"Excellent. You're back." Milton stepped away from the register, pulling a notepad with him and scribbling a note to her. *Offered a buy five, get one free on used books to anyone looking uncertain.*

As if rabbits, the store bags seemed to breed new customers. Every time one left, two came in. Not all bought, but more came, and all stayed a little longer than usual. It might just work. She'd have to let him do whatever he wanted. It could always be put back the old way.

Each time Milton removed another row of books, piled most in banker's boxes, and kept going, that attempt at resolve wavered. Her father hadn't been subject to panic attacks, but he might be now. With only two rows on the bottom of one tall shelf, she watched Milton swivel it to stand next to another on the wall and nearly gasped. *If we move that other one out of the way, Dad could come in here in his chair.*

Between customers, she met his gaze and mouthed, "*Thank you.*"

The placid, almost nonchalant air about him vanished, and in its wake, Ced caught a glimpse of a side of Milton she doubted many ever saw. *Delight. That's what it is. Delight.*

A familiar bus driver popped her head in the door and called out, "Fifteen-minute warning. An Uber to Indio will cost you a hundred dollars, so don't be late."

As if you'd ever leave even one of your most difficult people behind.

When the last jangle of the doorbell signaled the end of the rush, Ced peeked at the day's sales and swallowed hard. It wouldn't satisfy most bookstores, but one like theirs, with low overhead and a steady stream of tourists... If it kept up, they'd make it.

"Any better today?"

"As if you didn't know."

"It's a serious question."

He moved to lean against the counter, gazing at her with eyes that seemed to pierce through her and expose... what? She had nothing to hide. Or did she?

"You're an accountant. You know the bus routes. Is it truly any better today, or did sales show too great of an anomaly?"

This guy really does know his stuff. "If we can get people in... encourage them to stay a bit longer, it'll be more than enough." Much more.

There it was again. Delight—an actual twinkle in his eye. Milton pushed back against the counter and stretched. How did a guy in charcoal chinos and an oxford shirt do heavy lifting and moving and still look as fresh as when he walked into the store? "Perfect. Since we should be left alone for a bit, I think I'll let Atticus out of his cage."

He locked the front door and moved behind Ced. How had she missed a rather large, old-fashioned bird cage in the corner behind the counter? Milton opened the door and went back to work, pushing his tiny wire-rimmed glasses up on his nose and... whistling?

"Do you think we can?" Ced moved to help redistribute books and remove shelves. "Do you think we can draw people in *and* encourage them to buy more?"

"'Where is human nature so weak as in the bookstore?'"

She laughed. "Maybe *your* human nature, but what about the rest of mankind?"

"Henry Ward Beecher said it, so it was as true then as I believe it is now. We just need to ensure your store has everything it needs to loosen the purse strings."

That sounded ominous. "Such as…"

"There are lists under the register. Oh, and a receipt for the canopies I purchased from Amazon. They'll be here tomorrow. Next day shipping—and so-called free!"

"At least someone understands that there's nothing free about shipping—ever." Despite her flippant tone, nerves took over as she pulled out several sheets of paper. On top, a receipt for a hundred thirty dollars—four canopies for the patio. She'd expected it to be many times that.

The next one was for a list of children's books—both titles and suggestions for finding them. *Picture books about the desert, youth guides to national parks, latest releases, classics…* "Why all these children's books?" The next page showed children's toy and T-shirt suggestions. "Toys?"

"Half of the people on those buses are seniors. That means they're likely grandparents. Grandparents love to spoil grandchildren. Not only that, but just *seeing* something for a child will prompt a bit of guilt—a subtle hint that says they're spending time on themselves instead of with those grandkids. That inspires shopping. And parents like it when grandparents buy things they can justify as 'educational'—something grandparents also know."

The next two sheets were printouts of what looked like national chain bookseller shelves. "What

40

are these pictures?"

"You need to find out who the publishers of those outward facing books are. You then need to order what's next on their catalog of releases— preferably by looking at the store's 'coming soon' lists. You need three copies of each one."

That made no sense. He kept taking all the duplicates and triplicates and putting them in the banker boxes. Before she could ask about it, someone banged on the door. A glance at Milton showed him drooping a little before moving to retrieve Atticus.

"It's Marcus," he said.

I thought you liked him. Strange.

four

His truck rode a bit low as Marcus rolled into town just past eight-thirty that night. Gordon's truck sat parked in front of the S&L, and a slow pass showed the back empty. Why Ceddie needed paving stones, he couldn't imagine, but his aching back pointed out that they'd both know soon enough.

She must have been waiting for him, because the moment he pulled up to the back door, it flung open and she raced out, the flat dolly they used to move books around dragging behind her. A moment later, Milton appeared. *Oh, great.*

It wasn't fair. From what Ced had told him, the guy was some hotshot consultant who saved companies from bankruptcy or takeovers. That sounded like he knew his business, but if that were the case, what was he doing trying to save a rundown bookstore in podunk California? People just don't give away valuable advice. *Unless they want to impress someone.*

Ced reached for his tailgate, but Milton stopped her. "I'll get this. You guys go get the couches."

Couches?

She turned to him. "Do you have time to help me carry out Dad's couches?"

"What're you going to sit on?"

"I have my old beanbag chair from when I was a kid. Dad has his recliner. It'll work."

Even as he followed her to the truck, Marcus decided that they'd both lost their minds. *Nope… all three of us.*

They'd driven halfway out to the small, wind-battered mobile home before Marcus mustered the courage to ask about it all. *You're a LEO, and you can't even ask a simple question. Pathetic.*

"So, what're the couches for?"

"Get people in to sit and cool off. I called Lupe over at the Yucca, and they're getting the buzzers. Having a place for people to go to cool off means they're less likely to give up and just leave, taking those buzzers with them. So, they're willing to risk it now."

It made no sense. "You can fit maybe five people on those couches—if they're willing to get up close and personal with strangers. How's that going to help?"

"We have six picnic tables on the old patio. That's where the paving stones are going—between those tables. The concrete is in pretty bad shape, so Milton thought we should use pavers to create walkways on top to make a smoother path."

He might have argued, but she began talking—telling about the day's sales, the people's enthusiasm, the soda business, the ice machine she'd found in Indio that she needed to pick up the next day… So many things. So many changes. *Make the store pay off, and you can go back to San Diego.* The thought alone made him want to pound something.

"Did it occur to you that this could be a fluke? You could put all this money out there for something that doesn't work? Your dad—"

"Needs a way to stay here. This is that way. This store means *so* much to Dad."

"I know." That was the problem. It meant a ton to Gordon, but no matter how fondly Ced spoke of it, Gordon had admitted she'd raced out of there as soon as she could. Not that he blamed her. Not really. There wasn't anything for an accountant in Tamarisk.

"What does your dad say about all this?"

Triumph melded with guilt as Ced deflated. "It's hard for him. I promised I'd put it all back how it was if there isn't consistent improvement after three months."

"Has he seen it?" To give himself time to deal with the disappointment, Marcus climbed from the truck and went to let down the tailgate.

Ced followed. "We're going to take him down after it's all done. Just being able to move his wheelchair through there will be huge. He can spend part of the day at the store again. I think that'll help him recover faster than anything."

And get you out of here faster. He was a fool. He'd known the minute he'd met Mercedes that he'd fall in love with her. Forget that, Gordon had done his part to ensure Marcus' undying devotion before he'd ever met the woman.

The tailgate banged down, and Marcus stomped off to the front door. They usually used the back, but he'd have to haul the things out that way. Those couches would never make it through the kitchen.

"Marcus? What's wrong?"

"You're tearing up your father's life and you ask me what's wrong? Let's get this over with."

"Marcus!"

He pushed through the front door and nodded at Gordon reclining in the chair. "Hey, Gordie."

"Gordon."

"Have to try. Someday you'll see me as a good enough friend to give you a nickname."

"Call me Butch and I'm good. Call me Gordie again, and I'll ensure you sound like a kid whose voice is changing for the rest of your life."

Despite the bravado, Gordon winked. His gaze shifted to Ceddie. "Hey… What's wrong?"

"I don't know." Ced shot Marcus a look. "Ask him." She began stripping pillows and cushions from the couches and moving them out of the way as she grumbled something about wishing she were in San Diego where she had options.

If she'd seen the way Gordon's face fell… That only fueled Marcus' ire. He reached for the back of Gordon's chair. "I'm going to see if I can move this without you having to get up."

"Need to spend a penny anyway…"

Before Marcus could ask what that meant, Ced said, "That's for public restrooms, Dad."

"Fine. Gotta pee. Is that specific enough for you?"

Anyone not seeing the grins on the Pierces' faces would think they were angry with each other. As Gordon struggled from his chair, Ceddie struggled *not* to help, and Marcus struggled to keep all the emotions in check. Only once the man stood upright and grabbed the hated walker did he meet Marcus' gaze. "Music in your heart, Marcus. Keep making music in your heart."

His heart didn't make music, it clenched and twisted until he nearly gasped from the pain. It was the first time since Gordon's stroke that the man had used that phrase to remind him to keep his focus on the Lord. *"Sing and make music in your hearts to the Lord."*

Maybe everything would be okay... even when he had to say goodbye to hopes he'd had no right to indulge.

He'd moved exactly three pavers before Milton realized he needed gloves. Marcus would probably scoff at the idea, but after two scratches already, he'd never make it. "These hands were designed for pens, keyboards—the 'manual labor of the mind,' as Dunne put it."

Thankfully, Tamarisk General & Hardware had a nice pair of leather work gloves that fit. "Small hands you have there," the guy at the register said. "Women's gloves."

Sure enough, there it was in green and yellow. Womens. Large. *At least they're large.*

When Milton just nodded and swiped his card, the guy eyed him closer. "You the guy helpin' out over at the Spine?"

That caught his attention. "Yes." As much as he didn't want to, he offered his hand. "Milton Coleridge."

Yep. The guy's hand was twice the size of Milton's. "Dale Monroe. Nice thing you're doin'. Gordon's a great guy. It was tough, his girl havin' to come back here—leave that job in SD."

It took him a moment to process that "SD." Did most Californians shorten San Diego like that? "Have you lived here long?" It had started out as a courtesy question, but watching as Dale folded those beefy arms over his equally beefy chest and smiled, Milton found himself wanting to know.

"Most of my life. I was born at Twentynine Palms, but Dad went to a couple of other bases before retiring and coming back here. He loved this place. Said, 'I'll live the rest of my life and die at Joshua Tree National Monument.'" Dale grinned. "He almost did."

Something about the man's words sounded off, but those last three words distracted him. "Almost?"

"Dad died in ninety-five—a year after it became a national park."

Though he hoped that a few good books on the area would arrive before he left, Milton decided this man might know a thing or two. "How did Tamarisk get set up here? I mean, there couldn't have been that much tourism before it became a national park."

"That park saved us. This used to be a mining town—lots of mines around these parts."

"What kind of mines?"

"Gold was the favorite, of course. Some silver. A few minerals and such. There were over two hundred mines over the years, starting way back in the eighteen-seventies."

He wanted to know more, but they'd be back with the couches soon, and Milton didn't want any "it figures" looks from Marcus. As it was, he managed to lay out the first path before they returned. Ced found him wedging the last piece in place.

"Looks great. I wasn't so sure, but now I see what you mean. We just needed to cover the cracks and fill in the holes so it doesn't make someone trip. Cool." She jerked her thumb toward the door. "Can you help us decide on a set up? I thought I knew what I wanted, but now…"

Removing the gloves as he followed, Milton also gave himself a pep talk on all things reasonable. Like the fact that she was staying in Tamarisk, and he was headed to Delaware. Like he didn't actually know her—just that she had been named after a character in one of his favorite books, that she helped run a bookstore, and he'd never been so attracted to someone in his life.

Attraction does not a good relationship make… and neither does distance.

One look at the cloud on Marcus' face, and he understood why Mercedes had asked. Something was off there. *She's staying, you fool.* Staying. *If you are even half as in love with her as I think you are, you should be singing like the angels.*

He would have been. Just like the hymn… "'…no less days to sing God's praise…'" And sing his thankfulness. His gratitude.

Milton sighed and tried to listen to Mercedes' opinions, but a new thought hit him. *Unless Marcus did say something, and she rejected him.* But he could change her mind. It wouldn't be the first time in the annals of literature that a woman rejected a man whom she later accepted. Elizabeth Bennet, Margaret Hale, Scarlett O'Hara, Esther Summerson… Oh, who was he kidding? Half of Austen's works and several of Dickens' held that theme. And if he weren't so distracted, he could probably name a dozen more.

"What do you think?"

Though he hadn't heard a word she said, Milton began pointing. "You want the loveseat up here with a wide space between the back and that shelf by the window. You want the other one over here..." Milton stood where he meant. "And you want a table in the middle holding stacks and displays of books. Leave the underneath empty for places for women to set their bags and purses."

"That far apart?" Marcus shook his head. "It's not conducive to conversation."

Good word there, bucko. Conducive. Milton shook his head. "That's not what we're going for. We want a comfortable place for folks to both sit and mill about. If the table and sofas are too close together, people won't be able to move easily between the books. That is the goal. People lingering. If they can't move and sit without being crowded, they'll leave."

The moment Marcus had shoved everything in place, he flexed. "Did you get the pavers out of my truck?"

Milton shook his head. "I wasn't thinking about needing to clear it out before I began laying some of the pavers. Sorry. Let me get that done right now."

"I'll do it. You play with your books."

That set Mercedes off. She stormed after him, snapping about his rudeness and the need to be civil. Marcus said something about her being one to talk, and the door slammed shut before he heard any more. Atticus chattered about something. "I'm with you, little fellow. Something is rotten in Tamarisk."

Marcus took off the moment his truck had been emptied, and Mercedes went to get them dinner. Pot roast. The Monday-night special. Milton did what he did best. He arranged the pavers and mentally rearranged events until he had a plan. If he could save a company from bankruptcy or takeover, why couldn't he save a fledgling relationship from failure?

"It uses the same principles, Atticus," he huffed as he set another paver in place. "You just have to find what isn't working, remove it, and show everything else in its best light. I think I'll start with her."

five

Tuesday, Atticus spent the day in Ced's shop, and Milton went for another hike through the park. *"I need to think… to plan…"* He'd looked and smiled at her. *"To pray."*

Pray. Jesus did that… hiked out into the desert and did some communing with the Father. Maybe it's what she needed. She turned to the bird perched on a little T stand by the register. "Maybe then I'd know what to do. I thought staying might be good… time with Dad, time to get to know Marcus better, time to try to save the store…"

The little guy inched closer to her finger and rubbed his head against it.

"Oh, need a head rub?" She stroked it, still amazed at how soft the feathers were and how firm the bird liked the pressure on its little head. "Missing your friend?"

Atticus flew up to her shoulder.

"That's either a definite yes or an, 'Are you kidding me?' For his sake, I'll take the yes."

A bus had turned into town. She'd learned to hear the slight shift in the sounds even as a little girl and even as buses became quieter over the years. "All right. Here come the invaders. You'll need to hop into your cage for a bit."

Atticus didn't move.

"Just say, 'Into your cage,' and he'll go in." Sure, he will. As the bus passed the building, she became desperate and set a couple of pieces of red pepper in the cage. Atticus chattered something—probably, "Sucker!"—and flew into the cage.

"I'll get you for that."

Did that bird just say, "Feed me!" in that oddly high-pitched tone again?

The front half of the store had almost been perfected. Milton had informed her of the gifty items she needed to order to tuck into spaces here or there—a small Jane Austen themed metal lunch box with stickers and stationery inside. A few bookish T-shirts hanging between bookshelves. Pencil cases. A bust of Sherlock Holmes. Eventually, they'd have a large children's book display right there at the counter, but for now, the more valuable books had been arranged with a chalkboard sign announcing them as "Rare & Collectible."

While waiting for customers to arrive, she stirred the cold drinks, put a few in a bowlful of ice on the counter, and went to move the banker boxes she'd been filling. The door jingled before she could get the last three moved. Instead, she stacked them atop each other, lids still unassembled, and shoved them in the corner. Dusting her hands off, she hurried to the front. "Welcome to Spines & Leaves."

"Oh, look—cold drinks!" The woman beamed at Ced. "I'd like two. Do you have straws?"

She did… but not paper-wrapped ones. "I have

54

some in a box in the back—we use them for ourselves. Didn't think to get them for customers, but I will. Do you want one of those?"

"Please! That would be great. It saves a bit on the teeth that way, or so my hygienist claims."

A man appeared and called out for "Joan," as Ced was taking in dollars and passing out cold sodas. "Got one of the first tables!"

"Joan" didn't respond. He looked around and then stopped at one end of the counter. "Excuse me, but did you see a woman with a bright-green shirt come in?"

Ced jerked her thumb at the side door. "I think she's out there drinking her soda. She bought two, so I suspect one might be for you."

A man stood at the back of the line, allowing others to go ahead, one at a time. Tall, broad-shouldered, intense dark eyes. If she hadn't known all the law enforcement in the area, she'd have sworn he had to be. But at last, he stepped up, and a big grin changed the "don't-mess-with-me" expression to an open, friendly one. "Saw some books back there in boxes. Are they new stock? Not checked in yet? I found a couple I wanted to look at, but I didn't want to move in case it messed up some system."

"Show me, but those were all on a shelf at one time, so you're good. This place used to be floor to ceiling shelving with barely enough room to move."

"My kind of place, but I bet it made it hard to see what you had."

If she'd had any doubts, that statement removed every last one. Even someone who loved a packed store understood. "Thanks. Our sales have grown exponentially since the change. Whether it sustains that or not…"

The boxes he'd referenced had copies that weren't as nice as the ones she found for him on the shelves. And as he waited for her to ring up four books, he found another one on the collectible shelf. "This…" He swallowed. "Look, I saw this on Abe Books for one-ten. You have seventy-five." He passed a copy of *The Vanishing American* across the counter.

"We saw that listing," Ced admitted. "But we decided that we aren't confident in our condition comparison, so seventy-five until we did more research was a fair price."

"I'll take that, too. Can you wrap it well? Paper and a plastic bag?" He grinned. "My dad owns many of Grey's, but he doesn't have an early edition of that one, and Father's Day is coming…"

Father's Day. Maybe that would be a good goal—turn the store back over to Dad on Father's Day. She could just work from the office once a week—maybe doing book orders and such.

As the store thinned out, she peered into the patio and saw Milton talking with several of the customers. Though he listened and nodded, he sought her out and watched her before returning all attention to what the nearby group had to say.

By the time the bus loaded up, he'd come in, greeted Atticus, and made a few notes. "Well, want to hear what I learned?"

"Let me have it."

He leaned across the counter, almost coming alive as he spoke. The quiet, bookish man exuded something new and fresh when he was in work mode. "The misters have to be done tonight. Seriously, that was the only physical complaint. It's still too hot out there, even with shade and a cold drink. By the way, I think you could double the price of those."

"Highway—"

"If Disney can charge four bucks for a bottle of water, you can charge two for a can of soda."

She hesitated and countered. "Two for one, three for two."

He blinked. "Two for... oh!" If his grin meant anything, she'd won. Even as he started talking about T-shirts and key chains, she pulled out the cardstock she'd used for the previous sign and began working on a new one.

"I made this flyer..." He unfolded a paper and passed it over. "If anyone turns in an entry, make them sign..." he pulled out another. "One of these. They're under the register. It gives you exclusive rights to the logo if they win."

The flyer called for a logo contest. Winning artwork would win fifty dollars. "Who's going to do anything for so little?"

"It'll have to be better than the guys gave me on Fivrr. So, I decided to go local. They're vested in this town. They'll care."

He pointed to the door. "Time for you to go buy misters. And call Marcus, would you? We're going to need him. My talents run to cost analysis, not pipes and tubes and pumps."

She bristled. "Marcus is..."

"Of the opinion that I'm here to try to sweep you off your feet—or whatever the young people say these days."

That caught her off guard, but Ced laughed anyway. "You're not exactly old."

"No... but I'm an old soul. And he's jealous."

She snorted. "Hardly." But then a line from Longfellow that her father had read to her often came to her. "'The soul never grows old,' by the way."

After gazing at her for a moment, he turned toward the back. "Still working back here?"

"Yeah... the duplicates. We're running out of room in the storeroom, and we can't leave those bookcases outside forever." The reply came as if on autopilot. Ced grabbed her purse and headed for the front door. "I'll go to Indio for the mister stuff. Any changes to that original list we made up?"

"No. Don't forget to call Marcus, though. We wouldn't want to flood the customers."

As much as she didn't *want* to, Ced couldn't help but think about Milton's words all the way to the city. *"And he's jealous."*

"Just throw it up there and plug it in..." Are they nuts? Three days of working on this thing, and it's still not right. My entire day off fixing water problems so tourists will hang around and buy books... so tourists can give Ced an excuse to leave.

His phone pinged. A glance at the screen showed Ced's professional look with her killer smile. The text message read, GOING TO COCINA CALIENTE. WHAT DO YOU WANT? AND CAN YOU ASK MILTON FOR ME?

Perhaps he got too much perverse pleasure out of the disappointed looks around him as Marcus scrambled down the step ladder and hurried inside. Milton rang up a few books, talking about the merits and demerits of some author named McMurtry. "It's

58

a popular book, but put up next to men like L'Amour or Elmore Leonard, it can't compare."

"Leonard? I thought he wrote crime novels."

Milton nodded. "He did. But he got his start in westerns."

"Milty? Ceddie wants to know what you want for dinner—Mexican with street tacos and such."

"Tell her to bring me her favorite." The man's gaze nearly ran Marcus through. "And it's *Milton*."

Touchy... Call him petty, but knowing a weak spot felt good. Too good.

The argument, if you could call it that, continued before the door shut behind him. *Westerns. The only good westerns are the ones in space. TV. Firefly. Now that's a western.*

Not for the first time in the past four months, Marcus wondered what Ced thought of something. *Do you like Firefly, Ceddie?*

This sort of self-torture would drive him crazy. He went back to his ladder, back to the tubes, back to the pump that tried to rain them out instead of cooling the air. "Everyone ready for either a cool mist or a shower?"

All but one woman, wearing what was probably silk, called for him to start it up. That woman bolted inside. He flipped the switch. The pump hummed, and only one tiny spot in the corner "rained" at all. Cheers went up, and Marcus lugged the ladder over to that corner to try tightening the connectors a bit more. The leakage stopped.

Only then did he realize that by fixing it before she arrived with food, Milton would probably try to get him to create the speaker "hidey holes" they'd decided on.

59

"It's almost unanimous, for reasons I don't get. Most of the customers who come in here grew up in the sixties through the eighties, but they all agree. They think pre-sixties is the most fun for out here—the diner influence, I expect."

With the misters in place, he could figure out how and where to hide the speakers, so no one stole them and so they didn't get soaked with the mist. The answer came to him the moment he laid eyes on a broken cinder block.

Yes, it was immature, but he couldn't resist bursting into the store calling out, "Hey, Milt! Are there still cinder blocks in the office—for shelving?"

"I think so. And my name is Milton, Marc."

It wouldn't work. He didn't care what people called him. Marcus just grinned and took off for the office. After examining the wall, he went out back to compare bookshelves, came back in, and went to work. By the time Ceddie arrived, he'd have the place rockin' around the clock—or at least during store hours. *I should be thanking the Lord for being able to help Gordon instead of complaining about this guy. What does that verse say? Give thanks for everything? In everything? The other way around? I'll have to look it up.*

A song Milton had been humming the previous night played itself on auto-repeat in his mind, but Marcus heard the words, too. *"... no less days to sing God's praise..."*

"I'll praise the Lord... even when I want to curse His son."

"What?" A woman blinked up at him and pulled her purse closer.

"Just reminding myself that God's goodness doesn't disappear when things seem like they're going all wrong."

Six

"Hey, Milton!" She only had a few more days with Milton and Atticus, and Ced had decided to embrace them with everything she had. *Thank you, Lord for new friends like Milton. I keep thanking him—praising all he's done to anyone who will listen, but You… You need all the glory and praise.*

Mercedes' heart sighed. *I could have fallen for a guy like that… if stupid Marcus hadn't been here first.*

Her head said she could choose to love whoever she wanted. Her heart stuck out its tongue and went, "Ptttthtt."

Heart won. Again.

He appeared, still in chinos, but this time wearing the rush-ordered SPINES & LEAVES graphic tee they'd commissioned. Tan with brown, green, and black printing. It looked amazing. *He* looked as geekishly amazing as he ever had. "Hmm?"

"Ever read Grace Livingston Hill?"

"*Miranda?*"

Ced wrinkled her nose. "Sure. Not her best work… ever read *Found Treasure?*" When he shook his head, she pulled the book off the shelf—just a cheap

61

paperback copy, but he'd like it. She just knew it. "Take this one. Read it, and then stick it into one of your little libraries."

The reverential way he took the copy and curled his hand around it, holding it to his heart—Milton understood the import of a good book in a way Marcus never would. *Do I like* Firefly, *indeed.*

"That reminds me. You said you liked *The Railway Children* when you were a girl."

"Still do. I reread it last year." She pulled another off the shelf and held it up with a silent "Have you read this?" look. He shook his head, and she passed it over. "My second favorite of Hill's."

Milton just accepted the book and disappeared. He returned a minute later with two of their older books. "When you're in the mood for something sweet and innocent, my grandmother had these on her shelves. I read them, and I'd never have admitted it as a boy, but they enchanted me."

"*Rosemary...* I've never heard of Josephine Lawrence. That cover is gorgeous." The second book was a bit plainer, but it too had a cameo-like portrait of a girl affixed to the cover. "*Patty Fairfield.* Never heard of this, either."

"After years of living in hotels, she goes to stay with her aunts for a season at a time. Through that, she learns what sort of home she and her father want to create when they move to a new town." He grinned at the book before softening it to a smile for her. "There's a huge series. I liked them all. Well, I didn't care much for the very last one. Silly, silly book." He leaned closer and whispered, "Do you know... I always wanted to be like William Farnsworth—a guy who appeared at the end of the series."

"And who is he?"

Milton shook his head. "I cannot believe I'm admitting to anyone that I read these silly books when I was a kid. But really, aside from the effusive protestations of love in one of the latter books, most of them aren't too bad. 'Little Billie' is who Patty falls for—eventually. A tall, big man. From out west." The man didn't sigh, exactly, but he looked like he wanted to. "Marcus is more like Farnsworth than I'll ever be." A slow smile formed. "Although, I bet I know more of Riley's poetry than he does."

What does that even mean?

"And if you want to know what that means, read the series—or at least... um... *Patty Blossom*, I think. Sappy book, but it does hold a certain charm."

She would have gone back to arranging a display of the vintage copies of Elizabeth Goudge and Grace Livingston Hill, but Marcus appeared, a finger to his lips. Ced noted the way he watched her as he approached, and reminded herself to breathe as he leaned close to whisper, "Do you really think Milton read a book called *Patty Blossom* when he was a boy?"

Of that, she had no doubt. "Yep."

"Why?"

It was a risk—a big one. But several things Milton had said over the past few days prompted her to take that chance. This time she leaned close, trying not to notice the fresh scent of shaving cream, and whispered herself, "Because whether they never admit it to anyone—themselves included—even boys crave a bit of romance."

"I didn't."

Could you have a panic attack over the simple

decision of whether to flirt or not? Ced believed she could—and was beginning to. At that very moment. "But if you had read bits and pieces of true romance as a boy, you'd have stored them up for when you dared to try them on someone as a man, and *that* would make it all that much sweeter."

He'd looked almost... tender for a moment. That was the word. Tender. But something she'd said hardened him again.

"And that's his appeal, I suppose. That he's a romantic? That he's in touch with his feminine side or whatever they call it?"

Imagine that. Milton had been right. Marcus *was* jealous! She could let him know exactly how she felt, or she could enjoy the journey to him figuring it out. The journey won before the battle began. After all, hadn't she fallen in love with *The Phantom Tollbooth* as a girl? And hadn't that book taught her that, "The most important reason for going from one place to another is to see what's in between"?

"I don't know what his appeal would be," she said after some reflection. "Maybe that he isn't afraid to figure out how to touch a woman's heart."

A spark flickered in Marcus' eyes. Was it interest? Anger? Curiosity? *Jealousy?*

It prompted one more musing. "Maybe he's figured out what so many men never do." Ced couldn't have looked away if she wanted to—not with Marcus' entire being focused on her.

"What's that?"

"Romance isn't just for women."

"Romance isn't just for women." What did that even mean? And how could Ced—*his* Ceddie—act so enamored of a guy she also seemed ready to say goodbye to?

The way her eyes held his… Or did his hold hers? Marcus didn't even know.

A late bus rolled in, obviously one of the times the tourists demanded a return stop on the route home. It happened occasionally, and it usually meant for a long, exhausting night. *And you don't work until tomorrow at six.*

"Um, Mercedes?" Milton called out. "There's another bus coming. I was just about to let Atticus out. He really needs a break. So, unless you need me, I think I'll take him home before the store floods again."

Without shifting at all, Ced called back, "Thanks for everything. Are you going out into the desert tomorrow, or are you coming here?"

"Here—but not until after noon. I think I'll walk around in the morning while it's a bit cooler."

They stood there, only inches separating them as the sounds of Milton gathering his things, picking up Atticus' cage, and shuffling through the door drifted their way. Ced broke the silence first. "He loves that bird."

"I guess everyone needs someone."

Ceddie nodded, trying to look away, but somehow, he managed to keep her gaze. How was that possible?

After a moment, she whispered, "I wonder if he has family. I should ask."

"Even if he does…" Marcus swallowed, thinking of his crazy family with four sisters, both parents, both sets of grandparents, and enough cousins, aunts, and uncles to fill a family tree with more branches than an old oak—nothing like Ceddie and Gordon and their "Joshua Tree" family... just a couple of short branches with a few spiky leaves.

"Even if he does, what?" Again, her words came out in a whisper, and that turned his focus from her eyes to her lips.

Don't go there, Mendez. Marcus gave himself an internal shaking and murmured back, "Even if he has a family, everyone needs *someone.*"

"True."

Did her gaze just flicker to *his* lips? No... There it went again! Maybe if he just...

The door dinged, and a rush of voices flooded the room. Irritation flashed before he could hide it. Ced turned away without a look back. A baker's dozen of thoughts flooded his mind, but one settled deep in his heart. *I hate that guy.*

It wasn't fair, of course. He'd given them privacy. The customers had broken through their moment. Still, Marcus knew he'd be working on that repentance thing as soon as his conscience drowned out his anger.

He turned on the music to the patio, and the crooning of The Platters began with the iconic, "Twilight Time." Marcus looked over at Ced and found her gaze on him, even as she pulled two bottles of water from the ice chest. *It's probably all melted.*

A woman asked if he'd get down two T-shirts for her. "Extra-large and a large." A moment later, she pointed to a crocheted tortoise. "Oh, that is so cute! Is it for sale?"

"Made locally," he assured her. "Malia makes all

kinds of desert animals. She's working on a Joshua tree pattern, but she hasn't quite mastered it yet, she says."

And off the woman went, chattering on about how she just *had* to have the tortoise and a business card to order the stuffed Joshua tree as soon as it was available. He had no idea if he knew what he was talking about, but Marcus said, "I think your best option would be to watch the SPINES & LEAVES website."

"Oh! Great idea. Well, let me have that one, at least." She giggled like a child a fraction of her age. "My youngest is just expecting. I got a Joshua Tree National Park onesie for the baby, and this will be perfect. We always buy something for the newest baby while we're traveling."

He suspected they bought something for every last one of their grandchildren—a dozen at least, he suspected. *Her poor husband.*

That "poor man" showed up with a crocheted jackrabbit. "Look, Jenn. Isn't it—oh! A tortoise!" They stared at each other for a moment, both looking a bit sheepish, laughed, and said in unison, "Let's get both!"

Marcus had never seen anything like it. His parents would have taken opposing sides. Mama always argued for buying for her children. Pop for the grandchildren. "You'll spoil them," Mama would argue against toys. Pop would buy every toy in the store, but if she tried to buy something for him or one of his siblings, he'd say, "They're old enough to buy their own things. They have to make their own way."

Back and forth it would go, Mama insisting,

"It's a gift! We can buy our children a gift!"

Pop would argue, "They're just children. It's what being the grandparent is for—to indulge when the parents have to be practical." In the end, they'd buy nothing and indulge everyone by Mama making too much food and inviting everyone over to help eat it all. Pop by chasing the grandkids all over the backyard, throwing them in the pool, dancing when the music came on, flirting with Mama…

I want that, Lord. I want it for me but also for Ceddie. She needs that. We need that. Together. But how?

By the time the last buzzer had buzzed, and the last customer had left, Ced looked worn out. Marcus went out to the patio to turn off the misters and bring in the speakers when "There's a Moon Out Tonight" began playing. He glanced back to see Ceddie smiling at him.

"There *is* a moon out tonight, isn't there?"

He nodded.

Ced seemed to wait for… something. What? "We could…" Disappointment flickered in her eyes and she turned away. "Never mind."

The song cut off just at them strolling… a girl at his side. It would be crazy to do it—asking for heartache. For him, anyway. But… "Hey, Ced?"

"Hmm?"

"I haven't been on a moonlight hike yet this year."

The way she *didn't* respond nearly sent him home, but after much too much time passed for his comfort, Marcus thought her heard her say, "Me, either."

"Thinking I might go tonight."

"Have fun."

Is that a "Don't ask" or a "He didn't ask, so get him out of here as fast as possible"? Marcus set the speakers on the counter and gazed at her. "Want to come along?"

The hesitation nearly made him say he needed to get to bed. Ced sighed. "I should go home and check on Dad but…"

"You can call before we go, or we can stop by…drop off your car…" Despite every bit of his pride demanding he shut up, Marcus found himself adding, "Come on, Ceddie. You haven't done anything for yourself since you got here."

She hesitated again, and just as he decided he'd be out among the sage and the creosote and the Joshua trees by himself, a smile flickered. "You really don't mind me coming along?"

Here goes heartbreak… Marcus shook his head and leaned close. "Wouldn't be the same without you."

"We've never done it before!" Her laughter should have sent him running, but he caught it and ran with it… *toward* her.

"Yeah… and don't you think it's about time we did?"

The store seemed to close in around them. The books whispered their thoughts to each other while they waited for Ced's answer. Ced just watched him as if looking for something to give her the encouragement she wanted—that she needed. *Come on, Ceddie. It can't go anywhere. You're leaving, and I'm committed to San Bernardino County, but we can have tonight to enjoy the what if. Isn't that romantic enough for you?*

"Is your phone charged?"

Why she wanted to know, he couldn't imagine,

but Marcus pulled it out. "Eighty-four percent."

"Good. We'll need music."

At first, all he heard was the "yes" in those words. Elated, he almost forgot to ask why they'd need that music. "Why?"

"'I can't imagine anything nicer than to sit out in the moonlight and listen to music—'" Ced winked at his surprise. "Virginia Woolf. I want to discover if she's right."

More book stuff. Of course, she did.

Seven

With Dad's knowing grin burning a hole in the back of their heads, Ced and Marcus started for the road, flashlight in hand— off, but there just in case. Bright and seemingly larger than usual, the moon lit the night sky and coated the desert sand with a silvery glow. Ced's soul sighed.

"Is it me," Marcus began, his words almost in perfect cadence with the crunch of his shoes along the road, "or is the moon extra-large tonight?"

That did it. Ced whipped out her phone and tapped in the words. Full moon... May... yep. There it was. "Supermoon. Fifteen percent bigger and... no, fifteen percent *brighter*, and seven... oh, it'll turn rust colored," she whispered. "It's a blood moon. And at one forty-five, there'll be an eclipse." Unable to help herself, Ced began setting an alarm.

"What're you doing?"

"I don't want to miss it."

Marcus stopped there in the middle of the dirt road that led either to the highway or to the wash if you knew where it branched off into a biker trail. "Let's stay out, then. Watch it." Word by word, his voice grew quieter, softer, deeper. "Together."

"You have to work in the morning, don't you?"

"Yeah." He said it like, "So what?"

She could have said, "So… unlike you, I can sleep on the job tomorrow—between buses, anyway. You sleep on the job, and I have to close the shop to attend a funeral." And when she thought about it, and the grin it would produce, she did.

He nudged her shoulder. "Wouldn't want to do that to you, but I'll be all right."

"We'll have to circle around for a couple more water bottles."

"Sounds good to me," Marcus agreed. "Maybe a blanket." Then he made another suggestion. "We could hike over by Eagle Mountain and see it from higher up."

Eagle Mountain. There was a ghost town near there… four hundred abandoned buildings—twice the size of Tamarisk at its largest. *It could have been us. But we had Rice Road taking the buses right past, and they had only the iron mines.*

When Ced didn't respond, he asked, "Sound okay to you?"

"Yes, sorry. As long as the guard isn't around. I've heard of kids getting run off." This time, Ced nudged him. "Then again, maybe being with someone from the sheriff's department will get me closer."

"Those kids are trying to sneak onto Eagle Mountain property instead of hike around it. That's the difference. And Ed does his job well. With the sand pits and dilapidated buildings…"

Sand pits. She'd forgotten about those. "How about taking Coxcomb Monument Road toward the edge of the park. The hills there are good enough." Ced took his lack of argument as agreement and began walking again.

The desert has a quiet all its own. Like most places in the world, there's never true silence. The rustle of a creosote as a rabbit shoots through it, the whisper of its branches as the wind passes, the cooing of doves. Crickets.

"We won't see many snakes," Marcus mused.

"Thank goodness for that."

Somewhere a coyote howled, and a moment later, a scream ripped through the air. Ced jumped in spite of herself. "Stupid mountain lions."

"Sounds like that coyote is about to become lunch." He pointed at the bike trail. "Down to the wash?"

Where else? Ced just veered off in reply. A kangaroo rat dashed past, and a moment later, several bunnies scattered. As the next mini gust of night wind blew past, all of Ced's uncertainties and stresses flew off with it. "I love the desert at night." She reached out and brushed her fingertips across the tiny, white fluffballs of a creosote. "The scents... the sounds..."

With just a gentle breeze, a giant moon overhead, and nothing but desert wildlife to chaperone, it should have been the most romantic setting she could ask for. She'd given Marcus every out possible, and he hadn't taken one. And yet...

"It's a harsh, unyielding place. Mama thinks I'm nuts for working here instead of nearer the city."

"Riverside County?"

He nodded. "It's a bit greener that way. Not much cooler, but still. I just love the ruggedness, the peace, being forced to hold out against the odds that

73

it'll consume me if I'm not careful.

"But that's not true!" Ced stopped and faced him, grinning. "Louis L'Amour said so."

He dropped his hands to non-existent hips and gazed at her. If he looked at would-be criminals like that, they'd never dare break the law. "You're telling me this is the land of growth and lushness? A land that'll provide everything you need to stay alive?"

"No... but that's not what you said. You said it'll consume you, and L'Amour said, 'The desert preserves. What other lands destroy, the desert keeps.'" She fought for the entire quote, but it dashed off on the back of a cottontail. "Dad could remember how the rest goes, but it's something like how the desert preserves and mummifies instead of allowing decay and rot."

"And yet you still die."

"But you're not *consumed*. You're preserved."

"Kind of like down in San Diego. You're preserved in saltwater down there."

She sighed. "If the people and the cost don't smother you, first."

If it were any cooler, she'd have pulled on her thin hoodie, but the temperature needed to drop just a bit more. As it was, she started to feel a bit chilled. If she put it on, it would be too warm. The vagaries of desert life. Instead, she walked along, arms swinging, trying to push down the feeling of being fifteen again and hoping the boy would try to hold her hand.

Do you ever get past that awkward feeling? When do you grow up enough to go, "I want to hold his hand, so I'll just do it?" The answer was as elusive as so many in her life. *Just do it. Grow up and do it. Why not? It can't be any*

74

worse than this endless pretense we're both clutching.

Ced had just about worked up the nerve when Marcus asked, "So, when do you go back?"

"Back?"

"To your job?"

"Oh…" Ced fought to regain her resolve, but it slithered away and down a snake hole beneath a nearby creosote. "I have to be at a meeting in two weeks."

Marcus jammed his hands in his pockets and his jaw… she watched the twitch in it as he stomped through to the wash and jumped down. Ced followed, her own ire rising to match his. And for what? Why was he so annoyed? Was she supposed to just quit her job altogether? Try to support both her father and herself through the store and what, a few private accounts? Really?

When she landed with a soft, *whoomp,* Marcus was waiting. "Do you really think your dad is ready to be left alone like that? Who will take care of the—? Never mind." He turned away, heading down the wash back toward their house. "None of my business."

She took a risk of losing her job to come help Gordon. She's not going to take off for San Diego if he's not ready. But was he? Was Gordon really ready to take over the store again? Maybe one of the local kids would be able to work there when school let out. Just a couple of weeks…

I could take my vacation if Gabi would push it through fast enough. Two weeks off, and if Gordon isn't ready by then, maybe Lupe's daughter could... Anger boiled over as Marcus jumped into the wash to keep himself from saying what he shouldn't. *He's not ready!* A ghost of a whisper in his heart shot back, You're *not ready.*

"Marcus?"

"This way."

"*Mar*cus..."

Go for it. Just show her. Maybe she'll change her mind, but even if not... you'll have a memory. Right? He'd have a memory. And a heart full of disappointment, but hey. He'd have a memory. "Can I hold your hand?"

Where had that come from? *You sound five.*

Her fingers slipped over his hand and laced with his. It was the awkwardest thing he'd ever felt—that palm resting atop his hand instead of pressed against his own. *But it's a nice awkward.*

"Why are you so angry?"

"Angry?" That hand squeezed his, and Marcus realized the flaw in her hand-holding style. He couldn't squeeze back.

A sigh reached him half a second before Ceddie said, "Marcus, you're ready to bite my head off, and I don't even get why."

"You're leaving him."

She shrugged. "It's just one day. I'll take off early Friday morning—try to miss rush hour, but well... we know how that works. I'll be able to leave before three, so I should be out of the area before the worst begins—before the rush to Vegas."

A Friday. Her first day back was a Friday. That'd be good. Ease into things. He tugged his hand free, and her exasperated huff hit just as he laced their fingers together as they should be—where he could use his to try to convey just a hint of how he felt.

76

What would she say if he admitted that he'd been annoyed at how much Gordon talked about her? That he had been convinced he'd find her annoying just out of sheer self-preservation? Her father had spent months talking her up to him, and when he'd finally met her… *Well, at least it wasn't love at first sight. There's that.*

Four months of almost-daily interaction, on the other hand… *Who are you kidding? You fell for her by the end of the first week.*

"Dad can call you, can't he?"

The question ripped him out of his thoughts and pasted him back in the moment. "Call?"

"If he needs anything while I'm gone? It's only a day, but it's also three hours away."

The night wind worked its way beneath that paste and tried to free him back to his thoughts. "Sure…" When she shot a look at him, he said, "It'll be a good way to ease him into work. I'll bring him down at opening and stop by to bring him lunch."

This time when she squeezed his hand, she also leaned closer. "Have we thanked you?" He hadn't had a chance to process the moment before she said, "Can I confess something?"

"Sure." *Way to rock the extensive vocabulary.* In a bid to make himself look a little less pathetic, he threw a smile her way that he hoped wasn't half-hidden in shadows.

"Dad used to talk about you—all. the. time. Seriously, one of the first things I thought of when I pulled into the hospital parking lot was, 'If that deputy is there, I'll scream.'" She stopped short and listened. "Do you hear that?"

He did. He clicked on the flashlight and saw

77

it—off to the left near the edge of the wash. A cluster of rocks and a snake slowly moving away, the distinctive rattle slowing now that it slithered with purpose. Marcus dropped her hand, moved to put himself between her and a snake too far away to be a real concern, and with one hand to her waist, steered her toward the center of the wash.

Then he couldn't resist. "I don't recall you screaming when you walked into his room that day…"

"That would be because he neglected to tell me how cute you were."

Cute, huh. That's better than obnoxious. Ced seemed to be waiting for something. "Yeah?" It sounded like a safe enough response.

"If you only knew how many times a week he said *something* about Marcus Mendez. 'Marcus stopped by with food from his mama. Man, that woman can cook. And he treats her like gold. Remember that when you go out with a guy. You watch how he treats his mother.'" She groaned. "Over, and over. If we talked about *chip brands*, Marcus' favorites would enter the discussion. Law enforcement? You have an opinion, and it must be right because you're the expert. If I asked if he'd ever noticed something in a Bible verse, he'd say, 'Oh, Marcus was telling me about…' and off it would go. I wanted to ask why he didn't just adopt you and send me to an orphanage or something."

"You didn't figure out he was trying to set us up?"

Ceddie froze. "Wait, he did it to you, too?"

It had taken most of his self-control *not* to kiss her earlier. Marcus just didn't think he had any left in reserve. While his mind screamed at him to keep his distance, his heart drew his hand to her hair and tangled his fingers in the silky strands. "It got to the point I couldn't stand to hear him talk about his 'Ced.'" He stared over her head, unable to meet her gaze as he added, "When he said your name was Mercedes, I thought he'd named you after his dream car or your mom's."

"Most people do."

Should he admit it? "I bought *The Count of Monte Cristo* the night you arrived at the hospital."

That smile that turned him into a carbon copy of some sappy romance novel guy lit her face. "Did you?"

"Tried reading it." He kicked at the sand and regretted it the moment it flew over her boots. "Sorry. Yeah," he rushed on. "Couldn't make sense of it, so I bought the movie—with Jim Caviezel. Watched that and then read it."

"That's what I tell people to do when they have trouble. The movie's better anyway."

Marcus clutched at his chest and staggered back. "What? A book lover admitting a movie is better?"

"The movie is more overtly redemptive." At his silent questioning, she continued. "Edmund Dante repents in the movie. They take liberties, sure. But they show forgiveness and repentance. You don't get that in the book—or not as well. While it ends with the idea of 'wait and hope,' and while you do see some forgiveness and softening, the movie shows it so much better."

"Wait and hope…sounds like something the Bible teaches. Wait on the Lord. Hope for His return." The words had hardly left his lips when

Marcus realized it would be a perfect mood killer. *Yes, here I am under an enormous full moon, surrounded by nothing and everything, ready to kiss the woman I might be willing to admit that I love, and I bring God into the moment. Only me.*

Except she didn't shut down. Ced rested one hand on his chest and watched him before whispering, "Seems like that's all I do these days. Wait. Hope. Pour out my hopes to the Lord." She glanced away and added in a strangled whisper, "And wait and hope some more."

"Right now... I'm just hoping that I won't wish I'd waited."

That brought Ced's attention back to him. "For what?"

He kissed her. What an understatement! But trying to put that moment into coherent thought? Impossible beyond those three simple words. He kissed her.

Ceddie turned away mid-kiss. Marcus' heart squeezed, but so did his hand when she grabbed it and tugged him alongside her. "I wish I were a poet."

"Why's that?" To himself he added, *And why did you break it off if you still want me with you?*

"To be able to put into words what just happened." She stopped, turned to face him. Unsatisfied, she rotated his body until the moon shone on his face. "How is it that two minds refuse to meet—to connect in a meaningful way until lips meet and forge a bridge?"

So... she's not mad. Good. Marcus pulled her close again, touched—no, *bridged*—their lips again, and murmured, "That sounds like poetry to me."

Eight

With the speed and precision—or lack thereof—of a machine gun, Ced fired questions at Milton. What should they do about holidays? How much of the inventory should be added to the store website? (That pathetic little thing she hadn't had much time to work on yet.) What social media account should she focus on most—Facebook or Instagram?

He threw back a question of his own. "If you're looking at social media, why not TikTok?"

"I'm disturbed you even know what it is, but no. I need one to start with, and I think it needs to be one of those two."

Milton pointed to the window. "Don't forget to rotate that display *every* week. The bus drivers will start paying attention and pointing things out. They'll say, 'Check out Spines & Leaves. Their stock rotates fast.'"

"Facebook or—?"

"Instagram. Start there. It has a huge book community. And get comfortable in front of the camera. Highlight a book every day."

81

Instead of her thumbs flying over her phone screen, Ced had her laptop out and typed as fast as he spoke. "Gotcha."

She'd been so focused on her next question, that Ced missed him moving closer—close enough to lay a hand on her arm. "What's wrong?"

"Wrong?"

Milton just *looked*. That guy could do more with a look than an Italian mama could with food or Shakespeare could with words.

A tear slid down her cheek, and Milton wiped it away. "What happened, Mercedes?"

"We went out the night of the supermoon."

"You and Marcus?" A grin formed. "It's about time."

"That's what I thought!" She pushed away from the counter, moved around him, and began straightening a perfectly straight table of books and gifts—themed around summer reads, of course. "We walked, we talked, we kissed..." She whirled to face him and ignored the arched eyebrows behind the tiny wire rims of his glasses. "Best kiss ever. He felt it, too. I know he did. We watched the lunar eclipse and didn't get home until the moon started to change to that rusty color."

This time, a chuckle erupted. "So... that's why you were so tired and *not* grumpy that morning."

"Well, he sure is. He won't talk to me now—just grunts." She slammed a book back down on the table and jabbed a finger at the window. "Who does he think he is? He takes me out to do my favorite thing, more romantic than anything... ever. He—" She choked back all the feelings she did not want to share with a guy she could have cared about if given half a chance. *If not for jerk-face Marcus.*

Instead of reassuring her that Marcus was probably busy with work, that he had to come to grips with realizing he'd shared feelings he hadn't meant to, and a few more of the things Ced had been trying to convince herself of for the past three days, he walked over to Atticus and held out a finger.

Atticus inched along the shelf he'd been sitting on—away from Milton—and refused. Milton pushed back, moving the finger close to the bird's feet, and trying to force the bird on—gently still, but definitely trying to insist. Atticus wouldn't have any of it. "Come on, pal. Let's talk." He thrust out his finger again, but Atticus flew across the room and landed on a SPINES & LEAVES shirt.

Milton shrugged and walked away. "Well, be that way, then. You can just enjoy your own company. I have my books." To Ced he asked, "Hungry? I think I'll grab lunch before the buses arrive."

Milton Coleridge, you can be a very strange man.

The makeshift ramp they'd constructed to get Gordon in and out of the trailer wouldn't work long term, but the stubborn man insisted he wouldn't need it later, so why bother? A little steep, a lot rickety… Marcus felt certain going down the actual steps would be safer. "You got it?"

"Yeah. Think I should do this a coupla times a day. That'll build strength faster than those stretchy things the therapist gave me."

Once on the dirt drive, he shuffled, lifted the

walker, and shuffled some more. Marcus got the door open and was ready to help with Gordon's legs, but the older man did just fine. Folding himself into Ced's Prius again? That would be even less fun with an audience.

Gordon's chuckles proved him right. "Never thought I'd see the day when you were squished into one of these cars the size and shape of a Vienna sausages can."

They'd made it to Rice Road before Gordon spoke again. "So… just how different is the store?"

"You won't recognize it, Gordie. Trust me. But if there's a bus in town, she's selling—sodas, water bottles, T-shirts, bookbags, toys, and books—almost everyone buys a book." Marcus shot the man an apologetic look. "You can see those books now. You couldn't before. There's space to breathe and, well, like Milton put it. 'The bookstore now has margins.'"

Until that last line, Marcus had felt Gordon's resistance. The man frowned, and Marcus tried to figure out why. "What's wrong?"

"There are two buses there. Where are all the people?"

"In the diner, on the patio, or in one of the stores." Odd how in such a short time, expectations could change. Before, driving down the street could ensure you got cursed at a time or two by folks who forgot the road was originally intended for cars, not as an extra-wide sidewalk. Now…

Marcus pulled in behind the row of stores on their side of the street and parked behind his truck. He hurried to help Gordon out of the car and rushed to open the back door. "She's so excited, Gordie," Marcus said as he helped the man inside. "But she's nervous. They made a ton of changes, and she's afraid you'll hate it. But you've made more since the changes started than you've made the past four months combined. Give it a shot, okay?"

"Why does everyone act like I'm opposed to progress?"

At first, it seemed like Gordon might eat those words. He grew quieter with each step into the bustling shop. Customers stopped by the counter, passed over their two dollars, and grabbed whatever soda they wanted on their way through to the patio. Others wandered about. All made room for Gordon as he navigated the unfamiliar space, his walker forging the path for him.

Milton stepped forward, hand outstretched. "Mr. Pierce! I'm thrilled to get to meet you before I go. Thank you for coming in. I hope I haven' overstepped—"

Clutching Milton's hand in a shake that Marcus knew could crunch bones, Gordon put a stop to that. "It's unfamiliar… I'll admit that. But it looks nice in here. Might need some paint—"

A chorus of, "No!" drowned out that idea. One woman with a twinkle in her eye and wearing a T-shirt that read, "Book Boyfriends Don't Break Your Heart—Much," leaned a bit close and murmured, "You'd overpower the wonderful paper and ink perfume in here. Just don't."

When customers stepped up to the counter to purchase something other than drinks, Gordon kicked into gear. He shuffled around the counter and nodded for Ced to ring them up. "I can hand over drinks just fine."

Where Marcus, Milton, and Ced all wanted to

protest, the mostly senior group took it in stride, talking, laughing, commenting on this or that. Most folks pretended they didn't notice the slackness of Gordon's face on the left, but one guy asked how rehab was going and standing off from the others, the guys swapped stroke stories as if war tales.

Ced ate it up.

One more proof that you can go back soon. He'd tried to convince himself that weekends would be enough for a while, but Marcus knew better. *I want a family— like mine. A crazy houseful of kids and a wife threatening to beat them all into next week if they don't get out from under her feet. Laughter from those same kids because they know she'll just kiss and tickle them to death instead.*

And he could see Ced doing it, too.

"She's amazing, isn't she?"

Milton's tone held that note of wistful longing he recognized all too well. Marcus nodded. "I feel sorry for Gordie."

"Why?"

Are you that stupid? Marcus tried to keep the question out of his tone as he said, "Because he's gotten used to having someone around again. When she goes back to the city, he'll be lonely."

"She's just going for a meeting. She'll be back. He knows that."

I guess you are stupid. Wouldn't have guessed it. Keeping his voice as low as possible, Marcus muttered, "And when he's fine on his own, she'll be back in her apartment, back at her job, and far away from here." *From me.*

"She's not—" Milton clamped his mouth shut, scrubbed his jaw for a moment, and adjusted his glasses before speaking. "I think you should ask her when she plans to move back to San Diego for good."

"Maybe I don't want to know."

Milton turned to him and said, "The answer we seek often lies in that vast space betwixt knowledge and knowing."

It was a game they played—the Pierces and people like Milton. "Guess the quoter." Marcus shrugged and said, "With a word like 'betwixt,' I'm going to go with Shakespeare."

A slow shake of the head. A smile. "Coleridge—Milton, not Samuel."

Since when did joy and despair hold hands? As the store slowly emptied, Dad took over the register, leaving Ced watching from the sidelines. In the corner by the window, Marcus continued to glower until she considered telling him to go home. She could get Dad back inside by herself.

Except it might not be true, and they both knew it. Would he overdo it? Probably. In his position, Ced knew she would.

Their gazes met, and if eyeballs could singe a person from across a room, his did. Heart sinking, she fled. *I shouldn't have agreed to work from here— shouldn't have told Dad. Should've left well enough alone.*

At that thought, she fled out the back door around the corner where a utility room created an L shape in the building. Privacy. Ced gulped in air and exhaled frustration and disappointment. *I should have kept my distance.*

The squeak of the back door stilled her rapid

breathing. Ced held her breath, waiting to see if Milton or… no, Marcus wouldn't follow. It would be Milton. The guy had intuition that so-called psychics could only dream of.

"Ceddie?"

Marcus.

A few crunches told her he'd stepped away from the building to peer out. "Ceddie?"

She whipped out her phone and flipped the camera to ensure she hadn't started crying—or that the hundred-plus-degree heat hadn't already melted her face off. "Yeah?" It came out more strangled than she'd meant for it to.

Even had she not heard each crunch of his boots on crusty sand, the extra heat radiating from him would have given him away. He couldn't be more than a couple of inches from her. Ced refused to look back. Her makeup might be intact, her face free of tears, but her distress still showed—her disappointment.

"What'd I say?"

What did you say? Are you kidding *me?*

"I can feel it. You're ticked—even more ticked than you were a minute ago. What'd I do?"

She spun, her finger jabbing into him before she even had a chance to arrange incoherent thoughts into semi-coherent phrases. "You. Kissed. Me."

A smirk formed. "Yeah? Don't remember you complaining."

"Then you dissed me." Her eyes closed, and she strangled a groan. *Did I seriously just say that?*

"Are we writing a rap song?"

"If this were a hundred years ago, I'd rap your knuckles… then your head."

"So…" Marcus did that hands on hips thing he always did—the one that made her want to check her speedometer.

I'm not even driving!

"Despite all evidence to the contrary—"

"Do you *have* to go all cop on me, even while discussing a kiss that obviously meant nothing to you?"

If you could have whiplash from a slap that never struck home, Marcus had to after that. "Meant nothing?" He inched closer and managed to do it without touching her. "It meant everything. And it's killing me."

Ced ignored the "everything" that her heart tried to sing praises to Almighty God over and zeroed in on the second bit. "'Is killing' is present continuous—currently happening." She tried to meet his gaze, faltered, and turned around before he saw the tears that stung her eyes. "Wrong tense. Probably wrong everything."

"No… that's right. Every time I look at you, I see your backside—I mean your tail. I mean your taillights."

As much as she hated herself for it, Ced couldn't help a couple of giggles. A glance over her shoulder meant to be a glare, but seeing genuine… was that anguish? He swallowed hard, and she knew. It was. Ced faced him again. "What are you talking about?"

"I didn't want to fall for you. I was ticked off at Gordie for constantly singing your praises, to be honest. But you weren't here a week before I knew you'd break my heart. Stomp it. Scatter it in the wind."

"Why would I do that?" Repressed emotion rumbled from him with the force of Old Faithful. *Wrong park, Ced.*

"You're *leaving.* Don't you get it? I can't go to San Diego County. I live *here.* I own a house. Here. My family is close… to *here.*" He bit back something else, more words caught in his throat, and she thought he'd bolt. Instead, he grabbed her and wrapped her in a bear hug. Self-preservation insisted she'd melt. Her heart asked what the problem was. "I don't want you to leave."

"If you're going to be one of those controlling guys who doesn't let his wife go to the store without him escorting her, then just walk away now." Then his words fully registered. Ced leaned back and gazed at—were those tears in his eyes? "Marcus, I'm not going back to San Diego—not to live. I'm packing my apartment and moving home until I can find my own place."

"You're stay—" He shook his head. "No… but your job."

"Doing remote work now. Just a meeting or two a month in the city. The whole company may shift to home working."

As if he hadn't heard her, Marcus asked again, "You're staying?"

"I'm staying."

With the sun finally behind the building and giving them a bit of cooling shade—*I bet it's under a hundred now!*—Marcus told her exactly what he thought of that. Or, rather, his lips did.

90

Nine

His Land Rover and trailer took up all the parking spaces in front of Spines & Needles, but Milton wouldn't be long. He settled Atticus in the carrier and ignored the bird's indignant chatter about the lack of leopard spots. "I'll buy you an iron-on transfer of the bookstore's new logo. How's that?"

Atticus tried to bite him through the mesh.

"No. Leopard. Print."

Milton would have sworn the bird countered with, "Zebra?"

At least that wouldn't clash with Atticus' plumage, but Milton wasn't secure enough in his masculinity to carry about animal print "accessories." The bird would have to suffer. "If you don't behave yourself, I'll pull out the black."

That shut the bird up.

Gordon Pierce met him at the door, only one hand leaning on the walker. "Hey, there. Glad you could stop by. Ced's got something for ya."

She moved their way, her silky hair swaying, her eyes bright and... Marcus had talked to her.

Mercedes Pierce positively glowed. If he didn't know better, he'd swear she must be pregnant. *Why do we associate glowing with impending motherhood? What about sleepless nights and no showers?*

When Mercedes wrapped her arms around him, squeezed him tight, and whispered, "I can't thank you enough—not for the store, not for Marcus," his suspicions were confirmed. She stepped back and passed him an envelope. "We can't pay you for all you did. Frankly, I'd never even offer because I know we can't afford you."

"It truly was my pleasure. My favorite things— saving businesses and bookstores. What could be a better vacation?" He waved the envelope with a questioning look. "And this?"

"Just because we can't afford to pay you doesn't mean we don't appreciate all you did. Save that. The next time you run across a bookstore you can help, invest in it like you did in us. Buy their overstock, replace a sign—whatever. Please."

He nodded, tucked the envelope in his back pocket, and handed over Atticus. "He wanted to say goodbye… take a last flight around the store."

While Gordon and Mercedes teased Atticus from the carrier and gave him loads of attention, Milton gave the store one last perusal. Seating… titles you could see and read. Stationery, souvenirs, sodas. Even since last night, changes were evident. Mercedes would keep changing the shop to fit needs. And wasn't that what it had needed. At the core, that had been the real problem. It had served its purpose once… but it hadn't adapted to changing times.

Lord, thank You for this opportunity. Some might say there's nothing eternal about saving a business. Others might argue that my focus is all off. But this store provides shelter from the heat, income for Your children, and a house for many books that offer encouragement to others. You are worthy of praise—even in the renewal of a desert bookstore.

A glance over at the Pierces choked him up. He had to go. Now. Before it became any harder. "Well, if I can buy a soda, I'd better be on my way. With only six days to get to Delaware and get settled in..."

He called Atticus to him. "Come on, boy. Let's hit the road." Milton held out his finger from across the room and waited, but his eyes were on Mercedes.

Mercedes had been caressing Atticus' head with her thumb. He sat there for one more stroke before taking off for Milton's "landing strip." Milton winked at her. "Sometimes, all you need to do is let them come to you when they're ready."

Sprite in his drink holder, Atticus on the over-the-seat perch, Rover running, Milton hugged Mercedes, held out a hand to Gordon, and wished them both the best of luck. "If you have questions, email. I'm invested here now. I'll do what I can to help Spines & Needles thrive."

With that, he jogged around to the driver's door, climbed in, and released the emergency brake. Time for new adventures.

In the middle of ringing up a stack of children's books—books she'd have to wrap next, no less—Ced's phone rang. She'd have ignored it, but Marcus' face next to the number was a bit too irresistible. She tapped speaker and said, "Hey, Marcus. You're on speak—"

"Ceddie!"

Something in the way he said her name stopped her—froze her. "Marcus, what is it?"

"It's Milty—"

"*Milton.* He doesn't like nicknames." She chuckled at the growl he gave her. "You just missed him. He left about half—"

"There's been an accident, Ced. Stupid car passing a semi."

Her heart froze, dropped, shattered. "Milton?"

"It's bad, Ced. You need to come. He doesn't have anyone."

"But the—"

"*I* need you to come, then."

The woman waiting for Ced to ring up her purchases held up one finger and hurried out to the patio. In less than a minute, Dad was at the till, the whole store shouted encouragement of prayers, good wishes, and "good vibes," whatever that meant, and she was off. "JFK Memorial?"

"Yeah. I'll be here for a while. No fatalities, but it's bad."

And with that, Marcus was gone—probably shouldn't have called at all, but Ced was grateful. Songs Milton had sung when he thought she wasn't listening, or hummed when he knew she was, filled her mind and car. The guy couldn't sing. In fact, it had taken a few tries for her to figure out that he'd been butchering one of the verses of "Amazing Grace."

"Father! How does that verse in Psalms go? The one about blessing You at all times? Praises of You always being on my lips or tongue or in my mouth—yeah. It's that. How? How am I supposed to do that?

94

This guy gives up three weeks of his life to help us and now, what? His car? His trailer? Are they okay? What about Atticus?"

She nearly slammed on the brakes in the middle of the road at that thought. It took a moment, but she managed to find a place to pull over and did a quick search for reported accidents. He'd have been going east... on the 10? On Rice Road? Her app told her of a three-car accident near the junction of the 177 and the 62. Whipping her Prius around, Ced shot off, hoping there wouldn't be too many cars piled up— hoping she wouldn't have to walk miles to find Atticus and his carrier.

After telling her car to send Marcus a text message, informing him she planned to come get the bird—*Please, God, let Atticus be alive*—Ced focused on the road. Focused on breathing. Focused on praying she'd made the right decision.

She slowed as a short line of cars stretched out before her. They wouldn't be there long. Most would turn around any minute, surely.

After a moment of hesitation, Ced made a U-turn and parked off the shoulder. Phone in hand, she jogged her way past car after car, all still running to save them from the relentless heat. That was one good thing about jogging in the heat of desert mid-day. No snakes to bother you.

Sweat pooled in places no one wants to feel it. It trickled down her temples, down the back of her neck, down her sides. Her shirt clung to her, and Ced knew her face probably dripped onto her shirt as well. A few people shouted at her as she passed, but Ced ignored them.

When she reached the flares, her heart twisted.

Her gut clenched. She wanted to retch—would have, if she'd had water to wash out her mouth. *I might anyway.* The semi sat jackknifed. A smaller SUV had been mangled enough that she couldn't imagine how anyone had survived it. *No fatalities, he said. Does that count Atticus?*

Milton's SUV and trailer were both on the right side, an obvious flip from going off the road and into the sand. *Probably trying to avoid that other SUV. Passing. Idiot.*

A highway patrolman appeared at about the same time she did, and he called out to her. Ced ignored him, running straight for Marcus who stopped talking to a man with a towel to his head and stared. "Ced? I thought—"

"Atticus! Have you seen Atticus? He was on a perch on the seat." Marcus still stared. "Can I look? Please? He's all Milton has—except some batty aunt up in Maine."

Marcus waved her off and went back to the man with the towel. *Probably the truck driver. That SUV driver has to be seriously injured.*

Heart racing, emotions tumbling, Ced leaned over the open door to the Land Rover and peered inside. "Atticus? You okay?" She looked for signs of blood… and found them—too much to be a bird's, surely. "At-ti-cus… here, boy. Let's get you out of this heat." Nothing. The empty carrier had been flung against the window. Ced wriggled and struggled to grab it, scratching herself on broken bits of tempered glass. Something sticky coated everything.

When she climbed out holding the carrier, Marcus called out in what sounded like an optimistic tone, "Find him?"

"No…" Ced choked back a sob. *Not even a feather. Is that good?* She walked all around the car, looking for any sign of the bird. Wouldn't he be? Or would have been. If he'd been flung against the windshield, he could have been stunned, but then she'd have found him… probably dead in this heat.

Where are you?

All around the truck, under the wheel wells, anywhere there was shade, Ced looked. Found nothing. "Atticus? Come here, boy. Let's go find Milton. Come on… come on…"

The fainted hint of a chatter reached her. Atticus? A bird out in the creosote? Her shoes on sand with a healthy dose of wishful thinking? Determination overruled sense. Ced started to call out and ask permission to climb down into the Rover, but she changed her mind. Bad idea. Very, very bad idea. He'd say no. He'd have to. And she'd do it anyway. At least this way, he could yell at her without losing face with the others.

"Wish I'd worn long sleeves today." Because that's what desert rats did at the end of May. Wore long sleeves to work in a store with an evaporative cooler instead of air conditioning. Of course.

Not only sharp, the glass was hot as she wriggled into the cab and landed on the squarish chunks. It burned, sliced, and scratched as she felt around under the seat, offering a finger, pleading for Atticus to come out alive.

At the back, under the back seat, nearly in the cargo space, her index finger touched a sticky, soft something. She scrambled over the back seat and landed on the side window. It broke under her weight, likely weakened already, but it wasn't much

97

for the ego. Peering in that little corner, she saw Atticus lying there. Unmoving.

No... No... It's too hot. No...

As gently as possible, Ced scooped up the little guy and fought her way out of the Rover. She snatched up the carrier and ran—ran past people who tried to stop her and ask questions. Ran past Marcus who called out, called again, and began running, too. He caught up in seconds. "Did you find him?"

"I think he's dead, but it's so hot. Maybe if we can cool him down. Maybe it's just—I didn't take time to see. I just have to get him into a cooler place. I know it."

"My car—"

"No. I'm going." Every bit of her wanted to stop. To kiss him. To beg him to hold her and tell her all would be well, but she didn't. Ced ran back to her car, started it, and blasted the AC. Holding Atticus in one hand, she unscrewed the cap of her water bottle and poured a little into the tray of her console. Bit by bit, she wiped it over the bird's body, demanding Atticus *breathe.*

"I can't even tell, boy. Are you breathing? Is it...?" She moved her efforts to the bird's chest. Maybe with it all smoothed and washed, she'd be able... was that movement?

Determined to trust, she began singing a song popular at her church in San Diego. "In the desert wind, my heart rejoices. Singing praise to Him we lift our voices..."

One dip at a time, she washed the sticky, half-dried Sprite from the bird's body, but Atticus didn't open his eyes. Twice more, she was sure she saw the little chest rise and fall, and at that, she decided to put him in his carrier and get him to Milton. Maybe it would help Milton to have something to think about. Or maybe she could take him to a vet, first.

"A vet. Yes. We're getting you to a bird doctor. Stat."

Ten

With Milton propped up in his recliner, doing his best to help the Delaware company avoid a takeover, Marcus tore lettuce leaves into burger-sized pieces and set them on plates. Gordie and Ceddie would arrive soon—and there they were.

Three weeks into convalescence and Milton could hobble about a bit with his crutches and the "walking boot" he wasn't supposed to actually walk on yet. "Ced's here!"

Milton's calm, firm voice carried in from the living room. "I have another meeting, so we'll have to wrap this up. If you are not willing to cut spending in these three areas, you should consider countering their offer and taking it. This is the only way to save the company."

The man on the other end of the video call had a whine to his tone as he insisted that Milton would say differently if he had just come as promised. Milton didn't take the bait. "Numbers don't lie, Mr. Chankis. You cannot charm them into compliance. Like it or not, your boutique-style setup is costing you sales. You're selling to contractors, not D-I-Yers. That makes all the difference."

"But my branding coach—"

"Failed you. Either he didn't ask the right questions, or you weren't honest. Either way, it's not working. Meanwhile, think about it. These three are non-negotiables. If you can't or won't make these changes, I cannot help you. As per our revised contract, you have seven business days to decide. Have a good day."

How does he do that? For someone who looks like a total wimp, he sure can direct a conversation wherever he wants it.

Milton's call from the other room broke through his musings. "Is there anything I can do, Marcus?"

"Sit there and heal. We'll bring you a plate."

The front door banged open, and Ced entered carrying armfuls of containers—enough to feed them all for a week. "Food has arrived as has good and bad news!"

Gordie followed, limping in with a cane in one hand and Atticus' carrier in the other. "Watch out for her. She's got expensive tastes."

Either the truck or the trailer is totaled.

Atticus flew across the room the moment Gordie opened the carrier. He landed on Milton's shoulder and rubbed his head against the man's jaw. Marcus, holding half of Ced's containers, watched with a catch in his throat. *If we got married, I could have a dog. He could go to work with her. Then again, if we got married, I wouldn't be lonely anymore and wouldn't need a dog.*

Something about those words jumbled themselves up into one thought he dared never let

102

her know. *Mercedes Pierce is not the equivalent of a dog.*

"I think I want to try to eat at the table. Mercedes, can you help me out of this chair?"

He just does that to get under my skin.

The table looked spread for a party. A platter of burger fixings, a bowl of beans, one of pasta salad, and one of cubed watermelon. A square dish with steamed corn cobs and another of grilled buns covered with a kitchen towel completed a feast as far as he was concerned. Glasses of iced tea—lemon for Ced and Gordie. Gross. Unsweetened for Milton—double gross. Lightly sweetened for him. Perfection.

Milton prayed over the food upon request, and Ced pounced the moment "amen" left his lips. "How'd the meeting go? Are they going to listen?"

"No. I'll get an email informing me they've 'decided to go another direction' before morning. The only thing worse than slowly bleeding money is cutting open that wound and letting it bleed faster." He spread mayo onto his bun, making Marcus want to retch. "But that leaves me free until my August job in Minneapolis. I'm thinking about going up that way as soon as the doctor gets me out of this cast."

As if he hadn't said it a dozen or more times, he turned to Marcus. "You *will* kick me out—"

"—the second I'm tired of having you around. Yes." Marcus grinned. "What's your next business?"

"A medical supply manufacturer. I've done the preliminary work already. It won't be difficult to restructure a few things. They want to keep from getting swallowed up by bigger companies, so they just need to become more competitive on their pricing. Cheaper doesn't always mean more sales. I think we'll have them out of the woods in six weeks.

Then maybe down to Florida."

Gordie looked at Ced and shook his head. She glowered at him and pulled out her phone. Gordie sighed. "Mercedes Marie—"

"I'm doing it, Dad." A few flicks, a swipe, and she handed over the phone. "So, I was in a Facebook group for bookstore owners and showed befores and afters of our shop and shared the sales differences—actual dollar amounts so they knew that a 100% increase wasn't a matter of a few dollars. Look."

Milton took the phone and read. Gordie bit into his burger and pretended to ignore the whole conversation, but Marcus leaned forward, curious but unwilling to ask. Yet.

Ceddie took pity. "There are at least a dozen people on there who would pay to have him come. They couldn't pay his big client rates, but he could see parts of the country he might not have gone to—and basically free that way. He helps stores, stores help communities, and everyone wins."

"A man has to make a living, Ced." Gordie nodded Milton's way when the man looked up from the phone and passed it back. "She didn't promise anything. You can ignore and move along. At least she didn't put your name out there."

While the Pierces sat there looking uncertain, Marcus caught the flicker of excitement in Milton. Perhaps three weeks together made it easier for him to read, but Milton would do this. Of that, Marcus had no doubt.

"Working with the bookstore has been my favorite assignment to date. I loved every minute of it. Book people understand each other. There are special connections between bookworms that might exist between football fans or movie buffs, but I doubt it is the same."

Ceddie reached over and laced her fingers in his… her hand over his like she'd done at the wash that night. "He's great at helping people see what is right in front of them—books or people."

Like some kind of benevolent grandfather—half the age of most, of course—Milton beamed at them. "In bookstores, sometimes people can't see the leaves for the forest."

Gordie and Ced cracked up, but it took him a minute to get it. It might apply to books—well, to be fair it was a perfect description of the store packed with so many books you'd never be able to look inside. But how it applied to them, he had no idea. *Still, he got us to talk. He got us to* see *each other when circumstances tried to blind us to possibilities.*

Milton held out his hand. "Can I read that again?"

The table grew quiet as Milton read, pondered, ate, and read it all over again. When finished, he rose and thanked them all for the meal. "I have a lot to think about, and my ankle is throbbing. I think I'll go lie down. Pray. Thank the Lord for new ideas and directions."

"You'd be such a blessing to other people—like you were to us." Ced's fingers fidgeted with the buttons on her shirt as she tried to put something into words. "I hated you going without really being able to tell you how much it meant to me—to all of us. What you did—"

"You told me, and you showed me."

"Didn't feel like it," she muttered.

Marcus would have spoken up, but Milton held

105

up a hand, his head cocked as if listening. "And maybe that's how the Lord feels when we prostrate ourselves over and over, thanking Him and apologizing for things He's already forgiven us for."

She shrugged. "I suppose. Marcus called… and then when I saw those cars and all that blood…" Ced choked.

He gripped the table, and Marcus wondered if they'd kept him longer than his ankle could stand. But before he could suggest that they let Milton go, the man spoke, a kind of bemusement in his tone. "Funny… I've been focusing on praise this year. I've never been one to praise others or the Lord—not naturally. So, this year I've purposed to sing when I can't offend people's ears. At least it doesn't offend God's. That verse in 'Amazing Grace' has new meaning for me."

Even as Gordie snickered, Ced asked, "What verse?"

"'We've no less days to sing God's praise.' Well, I almost did. Atticus and I almost ended our days here. The least I can do is live the rest of my life in a prelude to that eternal praise, right? Maybe that begins with serving others."

He sought out Ceddie—just as he always did. "Will you cover Atticus' cage when you go?"

They watched him hobble down the hallway to the guest room. Listened to the door shut. Waited. Ced spoke first. "Do you think he'll do it?"

Gordie shook his head, but Marcus wasn't so sure. "He said something one night right after he got here. He was really struggling, trying to decide on pain meds or not, and when I asked if he regretted staying now that all this happened, he said, 'Marcus,

I haven't been this *alive* in years. Maybe it's time I retire and start living again.'"

"He's not old enough to retire!" Ced looked at both men. "He can't be much over forty if that old!"

"Ancient," Gordie muttered. "I'm a relic myself."

"He may not be old enough, but I've heard some of his negotiations. If he's been making money like this all along, he's got to be able to afford to."

"I hope he does," Ceddie whispered as she rose to start clearing the table. "He loves books and reading and the people who love both of those. It wouldn't even be like working to him—more like breathing."

Six long weeks at Marcus' house came to a close with the man shouting, "She's here! The trailer looks great. You'd never know it plopped over on its side and got all banged up."

Ignoring his already throbbing ankle, Milton grabbed his cane and pushed himself out of Marcus' leather armchair. He'd miss that chair. A glance around the spartan room produced a pang as well. *I'll miss this place. These people. My* friends.

How long had it been since he felt like he really had friends? *Another thing to add to my praise list. Friendship.*

The repaired trailer and replaced Land Rover sat in front of Marcus' house, the SUV idling. Milton hobbled through the home, double-checking that he hadn't left anything behind and his cane tapping against the hardwood floors with each step. "Looks like I'm good to go." Marcus asked how the ankle was feeling, and Milton assured him it would be all right. "If it had been my right foot…"

"Now you can say you're permanently on pins and needles."

"That's a new one." Milton sighed and asked, "Where's Mercedes?"

"Probably making sure Atticus has all the treats he could possibly hope for. She tried to convince me that he needed a bubble-wrapped hamster ball for safety. I told her to stuff it."

Milton sighed. "I'd put him in something, but there just isn't anything safer than the chance to fly out if I have time to—" He winced and choked back emotion that he didn't want to show. "I forgot to roll down the window when I saw that car coming. I knew better, and…"

"You have less time than you think, usually. It feels like there's time to process, but there really isn't."

The two men locked gazes and nodded. "Last night," Milton began. "You asked me a question."

"I did?"

You're already getting nervous. Don't hold back, Marcus. Let it fly. Milton focused on what he'd spent the whole night trying to find. "You asked me how you could know you really were in love."

"You called it pre-proposal jitters."

"I found that quote I told you about. It wasn't C.S. Lewis. I should have known. It was Dr. Seuss. 'You know you're in love when you can't fall asleep because reality is finally better than your dreams.' That 'dreams' threw me. I always equate dreams with Lewis."

108

Marcus pulled open the door and gazed out where Mercedes fussed in the passenger side of Milton's new Land Rover. "Then I've definitely been in love for months now."

"Thought you looked a bit sleep-deprived." Milton grinned as he paused at the threshold and said, "Take good care of her. She's strong, but strong people need someone to lean on, too."

Marcus held the door and asked, "And who do *you* lean on?"

"The Lord has broad shoulders. He meant for us to have people, too, but until He brings someone, He is sufficient." Milton offered his hand. "Thanks for everything. I know you didn't like me at first."

"Jealousy." Marcus probably felt as sheepish as he looked. "It's amazing how much I liked you once I found out she loved me."

For the second time in two months, Milton sat in his Rover, Atticus on the seat perch, the Pierces waving, this time Marcus waving, too. Just as he went to release the emergency brake, Mercedes leaped forward and jerked open the passenger door. "I can't stand it. I have to know. Will you do it? Will you help some of these bookstores?"

Milton smiled. "What would you do if you were me?"

Without even a fraction of a second of thought, she nodded. "Definitely—do for them what you did for Spines & Leaves." She shot a look at Marcus. "And maybe you can do for others what you did for Marcus and me. Books and romance just kind of go together, you know?"

Marcus stepped forward and slid an arm around her in an obvious bid to help Milton escape. Milton didn't mind, though. He offered a rare grin and said, "It's always been my contention that books are the strings that tie hearts together."

At the end of Marcus' street, Milton turned toward Highway 177. Rice Road. Take two. Next stop, Red Wing, Minnesota. One of the bookstores in Mercedes' Facebook group was there—Twice Sold Tales. He'd see what they had to offer, help the Minneapolis medical supply manufacturer, and decide about this bookstore revival thing.

"Who am I kidding, Atticus? I've just changed careers, and we both know it."

The End

Author's Note

I have a secret. I never know a book's theme before I write it. I learn alongside my characters as we delve into whatever truths a story unleashes. So, when I began writing *Spines & Leaves,* I had the story planned. I just didn't know how the seventh verse of "Amazing Grace" and its lines about eternal praise of God Most High would possibly fit into a tale of two hearts not quite meeting and a dying bookstore.

After failing to come up with any plan at all, I

gave up and wrote the story. Once done, I'd see what I could come up with—see where the theme would fit into the overall plot.

Two interesting things happened as I began editing. First, I noticed that praise had appeared without me even realizing it. I'd find a line here, or one there with a few short words of praise-filled encouragement. Additionally, I'd asked my editor to note any places where praise naturally fit. She found several, but the best place was at the end when Milton joked about how he had almost *had* "less days to sing God's praise" here on earth (yes, it should be "fewer," but work with me here).

Now, those who heard him singing might consider that to be a blessing. In my mind, he really has a painfully awful voice. But God, to Whom all glory and praise belong, would have heard them as a sweet offering. And isn't that all that matters?

Here on earth, every day, we have one less day here to sing God's praise. But someday, eternity will wipe the countdown of time away forever. If that's not something to praise Him for, I don't know what is.

Acknowledgments

The Mosaic team of authors, and especially our fearless leader, Camry, have welcomed me into their group with such warmth and kindness. I'd like to thank them for the opportunity to be a part of this anthology.

I'd also like to thank Christy the wonder-editor. Editing the book on a short timeline isn't anything new for her, but doing it while sick and just after moving nine children a thousand miles across country, and enduring a car accident in the process... wow! You outdid yourself.

Finally, my JTWE launch team. These fabulous ladies pray for each other, encourage each other, and read every word I write as I write it. They keep me going when I'm tired, pray me through when I'm weary, and never let me get away with schluffing off! You gals are THE BEST!

The Mosaic Collection

Pieces of Granite by Brenda S. Anderson
Watercolors by Lorna Seilstad
A Star Will Rise: A Mosaic Christmas Anthology II
Eye of the Storm by Janice L. Dick
Totally Booked: A Book Lover's Companion
Lifelines by Eleanor Bertin
The Third Grace by Deb Elkink
Crazy About Maisie by Janice L. Dick
Rebuilding Joy by Regina Rudd Merrick
Song of Grace: Stories to Amaze the Soul
Written in Ink by Sara Davison
Open Circle by Stacy Monson

Learn more at
www.mosaiccollectionbooks.com/mosaic-books

Chantona's

Recommendations

New Cheltenham Shopkeepers Series
The Ghosts of New Cheltenham
Something Borrowed, Someone Blue
Ghosted at the Altar
The Bells of New Cheltenham
Five Ways to Chase a Moose (and other relationship killers) December of 2020

Thank You!

I hope you enjoyed reading *Spines & Leaves*, the introductory book in the Bookstrings series, releasing book one, *Twice Sold Tales,* in 2022. If you did, please consider leaving a short review on Amazon, Goodreads, or BookBub. Positive reviews and word-of-mouth recommendations count as they honor an author and help other readers to find quality Christian fiction to read.

Thank you so much!

If you'd like to receive information on new releases and writing news, please subscribe to *Grace & Glory*, Mosaic's monthly newsletter at www.mosaiccollectionbooks.com/grace-glory/

If you'd like news about my books, the ones that go free, or new releases, sign up for my own newsletter at chautona.com/news.

Manufactured by Amazon.ca
Bolton, ON